SPEAK NO EVIL

UZODINMA IWEALA

JOHN MURRAY

First published in Great Britain in 2018 by John Murray (Publishers)
An Hachette UK Company

First published in paperback in 2019

1

© Uzodinma Iweala 2018

A CIP catalogue record for this title is available from the British Library

ISBN 978-0-719-52390-8
Ebook ISBN 978-1-848-54755-1

Printed and bound in Great Britain by Clays Ltd, Elcograf S.p.A.

John Murray policy is to use papers that are natural, renewable and
recyc̄   ̄rests.
Th   ̄rm

For those who lack voice

Finally he said, I have word from—and here he named the dear name—that I shall not come again. I saw the dead face and heard the unspoken words, no need to go to him again, even were it in your power.

—Samuel Beckett, *Ohio Impromptu*

No it ain't nothing left to say.

—Oddisee, "Tomorrow Today"

Uzodinma Iweala received the 2006 John Llewellyn Rhys Prize for *Beasts of No Nation*. In 2007, he was selected as one of Granta's Best Young American Novelists. A graduate of Harvard University and the Columbia University College of Physicians and Surgeons, he lives in New York City and Lagos, Nigeria.

Praise for *Speak No Evil*

'A memorable book from an important talent'   *Guardian*

'The soul of *Speak No Evil* is the tortuous, exquisitely rendered relationship between Niru and his father'   *New Yorker*

'Stunning'   *Vogue*

'Tackling rage, gender and violence, it's a sharp burst of emotion'   *Stylist*

'*Speak No Evil* is the rarest of novels: the one you start out just to read, then end up sinking so deeply into it, seeing yourself so clearly in it, that the novel starts reading you'   Marlon James

'A lovely slender volume that packs in entire worlds with complete mastery. *Speak No Evil* explains so much about our times and yet is never anything less than a scintillating, page-turning read'   Gary Shteyngart

ALSO BY UZODINMA IWEALA

Our Kind of People
Beasts of No Nation

PART I

NIRU

1

The snow starts to fall just before Ms. McConnell's Global Literatures class. It is light at first and hangs in the air, refusing to stick to anything, and instead hovers about the bare tree branches shivering outside. I sit down across from the window with my back to the door like the rest of the boys. We all sit close to the door because of the walk across the Cathedral lawn to get to class and because no one wants to be the sole male body surrounded by girls. It never pays to seem like you're trying too hard. Ms. McConnell watches us remove our jackets and place our books on the desks. After the first week of the semester, she gave up on asking us to settle in quickly. Now she waits with one fist gripping her pen and the other resting on her hip until we're ready.

I can't pay attention because Meredith isn't paying attention. She always sits directly across from me with her back to the window and the row of pine trees blocking the view to Wisconsin Avenue. Normally she tries to make me laugh with her near perfect micro-impressions of Ms. McConnell's exaggerated movements, but today she is half turned to the window, her eyes towards the sky. I scan the room. No one pays attention. Some of us focus on the interesting trinkets from Ms. McConnell's world travels. She has spent time in Kenya and India teaching younger kids and older women how to read so bright-colored Kikoi cloths line her bookshelves, which host Guatemalan worry dolls and rusted iron bangles. My classmates think they're real, but I have a cousin in Nigeria who sells freshly made antiques to foreigners seeking to collect their own colonial histories. Sometimes Ms. McConnell burns incense and the room smells of sandalwood or cinnamon. It makes my nostrils tickle.

I see it coming and try to warn Meredith but she's completely lost. Ms. McConnell is silent as she watches Meredith contemplate the snow outside. Our classmates suppress giggles as Meredith chases snowflakes with small cat-like movements of her head. Earth to Meredith, Ms. McConnell says. Meredith starts and hits her knee against the desk in front of her. She yelps and winces. Everyone laughs, even Ms. McConnell, who asks, what could possibly be more interesting than our riveting discussion in this classroom? It's really coming down, Meredith says. Ms. McConnell finally looks out the window and says, holy shit, and we all laugh. Everyone wait here for one second, she adds before she slips into the hallway and the class lapses into uncontrolled chatter.

Adam and Rowan rush to the windows. Fuck yeah, they say almost in sync. I can see the soft flakes falling on the pine branches from where I sit. A strong wind stirs sheets of white in waves and circles. When Ms. McConnell returns, she has a pained look on her face and I know that she's thinking about what a blizzard will do to her syllabus. Rowan looks at her and says, class is officially over. Rowan, Ms. McConnell shouts, but he is already halfway out the door. I think, how the fuck am I going to get home?

You can come to mine, Meredith says as we watch the layers of snow build. I call my mother to ask if I should drive home. If you can manage it, she says. I text my father. He says to just wait at school but I don't want to wait at school. I have spent so many years waiting for people to pick me up from school. Plus I can drive now and the last thing I want is to wait.

The cars on Wisconsin Avenue move at a snail's pace with blinking hazard lights. The side streets are worse. Meredith and I watch from across the road as Adam and Rowan try to move Rowan's car from its tightly wedged spot on the sloping street near the athletics facilities. Its tires spin on the fresh snow before it lurches forward into the car in front with a sickening crush. Adam shouts, Holy fucking fuck! Rowan winds down the window to survey the damage. He drops his head to the steering wheel and screams fuck into the thickening white.

Or you could be them, Meredith says from behind her mittened hands. I say, lead the way, and follow her up the street as she trudges forward with her tongue stretched out to catch falling flakes. Her hair grows a white coat and then turns deep brown as the snow melts. She wipes her nose on her coat sleeve and sniffles.

I think she's beautiful even if she doesn't know it yet. She has large lips, a wide mouth and an awkwardly pyramidal nose. She looks like a younger Anne Hathaway.

You should probably kiss her, Adam said to me once as we walked across the Cathedral lawn. She clearly likes you; and honestly it's not that hard, you just move her to one corner of the dance floor and then put your mouth on her mouth, problem solved. Adam is super practical about everything. He's the kind of person who always parks his car in the direction of his house so he doesn't waste extra time when leaving for home. I said, I don't think it works like that. Sure it does, he said, that's how I did it. If she likes me, she should kiss me, I said. It definitely doesn't work like that, Adam said. Then maybe she doesn't like me. Adam smacked his forehead.

A crawling bus packed with miserable-looking people passes us, churning up brown slush in its wake. If the buses are running, there is still a possibility I can take one up to Bradley Boulevard and then walk the last mile home, like I used to do after OJ left for college and before I got my driver's license. It would suck to walk through the snow, especially in my sneakers, but then I'd be home. I stop. What is it, Meredith asks. Her whole face is pale except for the pulsing red at the tip of her nose. Maybe I should just take the bus home, I say, the buses are safe. Fuck that we're halfway there, Meredith says, no fucking way. I try to pull away as Meredith grabs me. She slips on the sidewalk and flails her arms as she tries to find her balance. Her momentum pulls us both down and we laugh even though the cold snow sneaks into my pants. Meredith is right. What is the point of wasting hours on a crawling bus when a warm house and possibly hot chocolate are so close?

Her house is on O Street set back from the road by sloping flower beds filled with twisted brown remnants of fall flowers and decorative grass. They flank steep stone steps. My mother would approve of its understatedness especially because it would remind her of London. My father has never understood the logic behind paying so much money for a small place filled with old plumbing in constant need of repair—even if your neighbors are the senators, cabinet secretaries, and the vast network of unknown but highly influential lobbyists who really run this city. I like the redbrick sidewalks and cobblestone streets better than the large lawns and wooded areas between houses where I live, and it's much closer to school, but I guess the grass is always greener. Normally these streets are full of tourists and students but today they are empty and quiet as the storm settles over the city. I cover my ears with my sleeves as Meredith searches for her keys. Any day now, I say as she kicks her shoes against the bright red door to clean off the snow.

Everything is always life-threatening, Meredith says as the meteorologist on television frantically describes the snow that falls around us. She kneels on the living room couch with her face against the cold window. Her breath fogs the glass. We have eaten turkey and Brie sandwiches because there is nothing else in the fridge and no one will deliver pizza. I understood the turkey, but the Brie with its hard shell tastes of nothing and I have never liked its sticky soft interior. I've told her about the things we eat at home, dried fish that I actually like and tripe that I avoid by hiding beneath the lip of my plate and she has made involuntary faces of disgust followed by an unconvincing, that's cool—I guess. Her parents were supposed to get back from Houston this evening, but all the airports have shut down, says the enthusiastic meteorologist as video of snowplows waiting on the runway at Reagan National Airport streams behind him. Do you want whiskey, she asks before she disappears from the room. She returns with a bottle of amber liquid and she pours a little into her hot chocolate. You can mix it with your hot chocolate, it doesn't taste any different. She takes a sip and a drop falls from her mug to the couch cushion. She blots it into the fabric and then looks at me. You won't get drunk, it's just a drop to help you warm up, she says. I'm not convinced. If we lived in France, she says. If we lived in Saudi Arabia, I say. I don't drink because I'm not twenty-one and because I don't feel the need to drink. My classmates talk about getting wasted at so-and-so's house during their parties on the weekends, but I don't really pay attention. The risks are too high, OJ tells me. You aren't like these people, he says, they can do things that you and I can't do. He never drank and his classmates loved him. He was voted head prefect. He was captain of the soccer team. My teachers still call me by his name. I reach for the bottle and remove the cap. I circle my finger around the rubber stop and touch my lips. The alcohol stings at first and then turns sweet, bringing memories of when I was four and my father had friends over to watch the Nigerian soccer team in the World

Cup. I noticed an unattended glass of Coke so I quickly gulped it down, hoping to disappear before someone told me not to. It was more than Coke. It burned all the way down my throat into my belly. I felt my mouth grow hot. I yelped and tried to spit out what I hadn't swallowed. The whole room froze. My father's face became an African mask with exaggerated eyes, nostrils and lips. Then he leapt across the room, grabbed me with one arm and clapped me on the back with a flat palm. The sound broke the tension and made Dad's friends laugh loudly. They stomped and clapped. It drowned out Dad's shouting at me, who told you to come and drink that, enh, while he pressed my body against the sink and made me swallow round after round of water from his cupped palm until my stomach couldn't hold anything more. I vomited watery brown bile into the white sink and all over the countertop. I haven't touched alcohol since then.

Meredith stands and stretches backwards so that her sweater rides up to show the bright flash of her bellybutton ring. She reaches towards me and says, Come with me. I follow her to a bedroom on the top floor of the house where the low eaves make the space feel much smaller than it is. The street light filters in through a large circular window and quickly disappears into the nooks and tight spaces. Meredith flops down on a bed with white covers colored orange by the outside light. We listen to the wind and icy snow against the roof while the treetops outside sway back and forth, making the room feel like it rocks unsteadily. I hold my arms over my chest and massage my triceps through my sleeves. I have been to her house many times before, but never this late, never just the two of us. I know it's every teenage boy's dream, if only for bragging rights in the back corner of the senior lounge, but I hate the way my classmates speak about girls and sex. Their voices sound greedy and untrustworthy.

Niru? Meredith says my name like a question. She sits Indian-style on the bed with her head tilted to one side. Shadows obscure her face but her fingernails catch the light every time they slide through her hair. You can come in, you know, this is where you're going to sleep. I step from the wood floor where my toes curl against the cold and my feet relax into a soft warm carpet. I drop to my knees against the bed and lay my head a small distance from Meredith's knee. Her hand hovers in the space just above my cheek, and my jaw tenses, then my back, then my legs and finally my toes but she doesn't touch me. She has touched me so many times before, bear hugs, steadying hands, playful slaps while running, but this feels like it will be different. She doesn't touch me. Instead she tosses her hair to the opposite shoulder and places her hand on her knee. I close my eyes. Why didn't you kiss me in the Bishop's Garden, at Homecoming, why didn't you kiss me, she asks.

We'd gone to Homecoming together because we just knew we would go together and at some point between twirling around to "Shake It Off" and bouncing to "Jumpman" we left the music thumping behind for some quiet in the gardens at the foot of the National Cathedral. There was no moon and only a smattering of stars above the city as we walked arm in arm across the green. Careful, I said because the high heels she wore with her short black cocktail dress sank into the soft grass. I held her hand while she removed them and we walked with our fingers interlocked across the lawn to a gazebo surrounded by carefully tufted and wilting wild grass. A few yards from the entrance we saw two figures caressing in the shadows, completely unaware of the rest of the world. Meredith slipped her arm in mine and we backed away quietly towards the flagstone paths that twisted through the rose bushes and wildflower beds.

It's Ms. McConnell, Meredith giggled when we stopped in the stone nook beneath the gnarled branches of an ancient evergreen. The warm fall weather meant the fountains still gurgled. An oxidized copper sun spat water into a small pool behind a ledge onto which Meredith lowered herself. She pulled me down next to her and swung her legs over mine because she said the stone was too cold against her bare thighs. It didn't feel cold to my palms. She took my jacket and draped it over her shoulders. She said, Oh my God. She was totally tongue fucking that guy. I searched for a place to put my hands. Meredith's strapless dress threatened to slide down her chest, but she didn't seem to notice or care. I smiled to relieve the burning feeling of foolishness spread across my face. Meredith tensed her legs. Her breath smelled of the cherry Dum Dums the student council had dumped into large bins outside the dance hall. She'd been sucking on one when we left the building.

Just put your mouth on her mouth, Adam said, it's basic biology. I put a hand in my pants pocket and hoped Meredith couldn't see me feeling around to make sure that all of my parts remained in their proper places. She leaned in closer. Then she snapped away as footsteps echoed off the stone wall around us. I saw Ms. McConnell first and then the man following her, holding her hand. Ms. McConnell's mouth fell open as she cocked her head. Oh hey Ms. McConnell, Meredith said. She slipped my jacket over her bare legs. You two know you're not supposed to be in here this late, Ms. McConnell said. She'd released herself from her companion and locked her fingers at her navel. I looked away from the skewed buttons of Ms. McConnell's blouse and focused on the dark moss in the cracks between the stones. Ms. McConnell quickly folded her arms over her chest. You should go back inside, or you should go home, she said. Meredith stood and finger waved good night. I exhaled.

Will you kiss me now, she asks as she marches her fingers across the space between us on the bed. She cups my face in her hands and gently tilts my head back. Okay, I say and close my eyes. Her chapped lips scratch mine. Her breath smells like hot chocolate and whiskey. Her hair tickles my nose. I breathe in and can suddenly smell all of her, the underlying damp from our walk through the snow that lingers in her hair, the turkey and Brie on her fingertips. Her tongue searches my lips. It touches my teeth and plays against my tongue before retreating. When it comes back it's more confident as the rest of her body moves towards mine. Her legs encircle my hips and lock around my lower back. She presses against me and puts her cheek to my cheek before she kisses my neck. I shiver. My hands rise up over her sweater, guided by her hands. Then they are underneath the fabric, my palms against her skin, sweeping up and over her small breasts and hard nipples. She breathes in sharply. I feel my heart. I hear the rush of my blood. It is this simple.

Here, take off your shirt, Meredith says. Her cold hands push away my turtleneck. My skin prickles. She removes her sweater, her bra, and slides her leggings and panties down to the floor. I have never seen a naked woman in real life. Blue veins trace up and around occasional moles and birthmarks on her otherwise pale skin. She's shaved everything except for a narrow track of brown hair between her legs. Her breasts are larger than I expected but then I've only seen her wearing a sports bra beneath her T-shirt. She smiles down at me but her eyes search my face. I feel unsteady in this room of shifting shadows. Snow crackles against the roof. Tree branches beat the siding and scratch the windows. She kisses my neck again. She kisses my chest. Her tongue explores my nipples while her hands fumble with my belt.

Desire is desire, our Ancient Greek History teacher said once. She is an older woman with wrinkles in wrinkles magnified by oversize lenses that bulge out from awkwardly thin wire frames. She took us to the Smithsonian to see ancient Greek urns painted black with faded orange men and women pleasuring orange men and women under the thrall of Eros further enabled by Dionysus. For the Greeks, pleasure derived from submission to passion, and passion appeared in many forms. Desire had no right. No wrong. It simply was, she said.

Meredith, I whisper. I step back but her hands follow me, still working against my belt buckle. I grab her wrists and pull them away. No. Something's not okay, I say. She falls back onto the bed with her legs firmly pressed together. No, she says, this is not happening. Then she is no longer in the room. I wrap my arms around my body. It is suddenly unbearably cold.

The white kids used to touch me all the time when I was younger, like they owned me. They'd call me Velcro Head and press things to my hair to see what would stick. I let them play around because there were always more of them than me and because back then I didn't know the difference between ignorance and malice. Then there was that time one of the girls came up to me after school and asked if she could look down my pants, just a peek, you know, to settle a debate they had after sex ed. I pretended not to hear, but I walked around the rest of the day staring at the floor with my fists clenched.

Meredith has left me alone because I will not give her what she wants, but what about what I want. What do I want? More than anything I want to be home right now with the thermostat high enough that I can feel comfortable in a T-shirt. I want to smell my mother's chicken-pepper soup, her anti–cold weather charm, but there is no way towards that now.

Meredith. I hiss her name. In the darkness it feels like soft voices are more appropriate. I creep along the landing trying to feel my way while the house clicks and cracks as it settles around me. I am cold and tense partly because the joke that the black guy always dies first seems too real in the middle of this rapidly accelerating horror show. Meredith, where are you? I try each of the doorknobs I pass as I make my way towards another set of stairs. They open into a bedroom, a study and a bathroom, all empty.

I move slowly because it's entirely within Meredith's character to play a practical joke by hiding behind a bed or a door to scare me. She has a harsh sense of humor, especially in difficult situations. Sometimes it makes things better but mostly it just creates more tension. (I'm misunderstood, she likes to say. No, you're just an asshole, I tell her.) Dude. It's not funny anymore. This isn't cool, I say.

I hear a sniffle behind me and spin around. The landing is still empty. I'm not trying to be funny, she says, but I still can't see anyone. I follow her voice back toward the stairs up to the guest room, feeling along the wall with my fingertips. There are no knobs or handles but my fingers touch a seam in the drywall. Where are you, I whisper. Meredith coughs. It's really cold out here and I think you have my shirt, I say. Fuck your shirt, she says, but I hear rustling through the wall. I'm not playing, Meredith. Neither am I. I shiver and rub my arms. What if her parents come back to find a half-naked black man standing in the middle of their upstairs hallway. This kind of thing never ends well for the black man, no matter how innocent. I really should have driven home. Any accident could not have been more of a wreck than this evening.

Meredith groans. I don't get it, you keep rejecting me, she says. She sniffles again as she works herself into sobs. I try to swallow but I can't. Meredith, it's not—I can't continue because I don't know what to say. I wish for a steady voice, for some of OJ's confidence, my father's single-mindedness, my mother's calm. I pinch my arms and dig my nails into my own skin and scratch. The burning is relief, the pain a welcome distraction. Is it my face, she whimpers. No. You don't like my body? No. I'm not cool enough for you? I bring my palm to my mouth and bite down against the fleshy pad of my thumb. I raise my knuckles to my lips. I'm not black enough? No. Is it my lack of booty? Meredith manages a chuckle. No, I say. Well what the fuck is wrong with me then?

I've asked myself the very same question since that first time something felt different when I wrestled with Zhou, my next-door neighbor, until his father got a job with an aerospace company in San Diego. We threw each other to the carpets and lay down on each other. I felt Zhou's breath against my face and neck. His chest moved against my chest and it felt nice with our legs tangled together.

Because boys aren't supposed to like other boys, my mother said to me when I asked what the pastor meant when he said America was living under the shadow of that abomination, homo-sexuality. But OJ likes boys and I like Zhou, I said. *Abeg*, leave that thing, my mother said. She only ever speaks pidgin when she's surprised or angry. Otherwise she sounds faintly British. She fidgeted in the driver's seat and turned up the radio so I knew she didn't want to talk. She said, God said man is for woman and woman is for man. That's how it's supposed to be. And God was always right; so I decided I would only like girls even if I could feel that I liked looking at them less than I should. I didn't watch the porn my classmates shared on their phones in the hallways before class or sitting on the lawn in front of the Cathedral. At home, I would watch women with women and men with women on my phone, trying only to focus on the women as I touched myself. But those men, their bodies, their sounds. I wanted to gouge out my eyes. Sometimes I asked God for deliverance. Sometimes I held my own breath and circled my hands around my throat and squeezed until they grew tired and I coughed saliva over my lips and onto my chin. Sometimes I cried. When my mother asked me what was wrong I said homework. She never probed any further. Sometimes when Meredith touched me, when she circled her arms around my neck or pinched my butt, I felt something, but never very strong or for very long.

There is nothing wrong with you, I say into the darkness. I slump against the wall and slide to the floor. I say, Meredith, I think—I'm gay. She slides the door back and thrusts her head out from the closet. She has wrapped herself in a blanket and her hair covers her face. She says, what?

She stretches an arm out from the darkness and lets it fall. Then she emerges and envelops me fully in her blanket. She holds me as she murmurs, I'm right here. She says, I'm with you. I start to cry. I'm overwhelmed by the sound of my own pain. She tries to slow things down the way our track coaches slow us down. Count your breaths, Niru, she says. Follow my voice, Niru. I follow for a moment, but my thoughts are strong and I choke on a mixture of relief, embarrassment, and fear. She pulls me closer and rocks with me. She drapes an arm over me and clasps my hand. She says, I'll always be here. I say, what do we do now?

2

I'm late, the kind of late that suggests I have no regard for the emotional health of my Nigerian parents who probably think I've been kidnapped by the enemies of progress. To make matters worse, I still can't find my phone so there is no way to call home and offer excuses. They will worry in their own ways, my mother sunk down in her red lounge chair trying to focus on patient charts or a medical textbook in her lap, nodding in and out of sleep, my father at the kitchen table staring with disinterest at whatever food she has set in front of him. But my problem is that they're worrying at all and that never ends well. For all the years they've lived abroad, they are still so very Nigerian. I can sometimes see the mental strain on their faces when they try to assimilate to some of the more grating aspects of American life. My father doesn't understand the desire to "hang out." What are you "hanging" from, my friend, he says. Do you think that Apple man made his money by hanging out, talkless of Bill Gates.

My father thinks the safest place for a man to be, especially in America, is inside his own house. He relishes coming home and as soon as he enters our kitchen through the garage door, his anger and stress fall away. He takes off his tie and tosses it on the counter before he grabs a beer from the fridge, and then he is calm. You don't disrupt this routine without profound negative consequences. My not being home will disrupt this routine yet again, especially since I couldn't come home for two days during the blizzard, and for the first twelve hours, my parents couldn't reach me after my phone died and the power went out. This is not good.

My own routines have been completely busted since I spoke my truth, as Meredith now calls it. I can't seem to remember anything. My body and brain feel numb. At night I lie awake staring at shadows that float across my ceiling. In the mornings, I forget to take out the trash and then I forget to bring the bins back up the driveway when I come home at the end of the day. Is everything okay, my mother has asked me and I've mumbled back, yeah I'm fine, but I can tell she doesn't believe me. She's decided to give me some watchful space because she's a very perceptive woman. She says it comes from having to communicate with the barely verbal and nonverbal children, unwilling teenagers, and frantic parents she sees every day at her practice. She also says she's a woman, that she knows things.

Do you think people can tell I've changed, I've asked Meredith over and over again, before class, after class, in our Snapchats long after we've gone home. Do you think they know, I asked her one afternoon as we sat in our special place beneath the but-tress. It was still too cold to be outside, but the start of track season meant the unofficial start of spring where people believe acting like the world is warm will suddenly make the world warm. She asked, has anyone said anything to you? No one had said a word to me, but that was almost beside the point. You need an outlet, Meredith said and plucked a blade of grass from the ground.

The new track season also meant a return to the crowded locker room full of half-naked boys and their banter, their bodies. I'm no stranger to locker room antics, hiding clothes, shower wres-tling, pantsing people, twisting nipples. I know that someone will slap or grab my ass and pretend to ride me. Now, I don't know how I'll respond, or if that response will be involuntary, and that scares me.

But you've probably always been gay and if no one has said anything for the last eighteen years then why would they say any-thing now, Meredith said. It just feels different now, Meredith. Before I said it out loud, I could pretend I didn't know, I said, but speaking the words out loud, I feel like I've let something loose that I can't control. You definitely need an outlet, she said, if only so you'll stop asking me the same question over and over again, and she tossed me my phone. The lock screen was filled with Grindr alerts and Tinder notifications. What the fuck did you do, I asked as I fumbled the catch and it dropped to the grass. You're welcome, Meredith said. You forgot your phone in Ms. McCon-nell's class, I just took the liberty to install a couple apps. You can delete them if you want, or you can check it out—it can't hurt, can it? She crossed her arms and stared into one of the halogen lights buzzing in its casing. I slipped the phone into my pocket. Come on, I said, we're late for practice.

At a stoplight, I rummage through a stack of old papers and cassette tapes in the glove box. I sweep my hand between the seats but feel only years of crumbs and old popcorn kernels in the creases. They stick beneath my fingernails, a testament to the earlier days when my mother used to drive OJ and me to school. She likes Volvos because her mother liked Volvos and because they are safe. OJ drove this car before he went to college and now I drive it. I'm forced to burn my music onto CDs because there's no tape deck and it doesn't have an auxiliary-cable port. Meredith calls the cracked black leather seats distressed. I dream of a BMW. I slam the glove box closed and try to breathe against a growing panic. I was late to class because I searched this car for fifteen minutes looking for my phone. It's now a liability and has been from the moment I didn't delete the apps Meredith installed. More important, I need it now to call and broker peace with my parents, but it's nowhere to be seen.

You can just delete them, Meredith said as we sat in my car after practice. But I've always been curious and there is also desire. I looked at my phone and felt the tingling creep, the stiffness rising. Pick someone for me, I said. So she swiped and tapped and picked Ryan with his short twists and aggressively attractive bleach-white smile. His profile pictures showed him suspended in various forms of dance, in various stages of undress above the caption Movement Is Life. Oh match, she squealed, see it's easy. Now all you have to do is go.

Ryan's avatar texted me the next day: we can have coffee and then whatever. I texted back, sure, completely uncertain of what I'd just done. Coffee I understood, but the whatever rattled around my head. The word sounded so much like the "whatever" Reverend Olumide railed against from the pulpit on Sundays. You have kids saying whatever, doing whatever, whatever whatever. And then they have boyfriends or babies. Yes. They find themselves experimenting with lesbianism and homosexuality and all manner of unclean things.

I am not unclean, I say aloud as I barrel down Sixteenth Street, but I'm not convinced. I haven't done anything yet, I say to myself, I ran away from doing something. Temptation must always come, Reverend Olumide says almost every service. Sin will never go away, he shouts, it's for you not to go toward it. I pick up speed. It's late enough that traffic is light and the remaining cars move freely. I pass our church and its stone lions out in front of the entrance, then the Carter Barron amphitheater nestled inside the woods of Rock Creek Park. There are fewer lights up ahead so I press down on the gas.

Maybe you forgot it at home, Meredith said as we walked down to the track earlier that afternoon. Our warm-up pants swished with each step and a gray sky threatened rain. At lunch I looked around at all the track team members silently praying for thunderstorms while we ate salads in advance of the season's first speed workout. I hadn't eaten much because of the workout, but also because of nervousness. Ryan's text beneath his smiling face flickered before me, coffee and whatever. I'm actually going to do this. Niru is actually going to do this, I repeated to myself. And why not? It was just a quick meetup, coffee after practice and then home. There wasn't going to be any time for whatever. I didn't forget it, I said. I could swear I had it with me this morning when I got in the car. Maybe it's a sign, maybe I'm not supposed to go. What if it's like God's way of telling me that he's a serial killer, or he has AIDS? Because the probability of both of those things is so high, Meredith said. Reverend Olumide would say so. Or you could just go and see what happens, Meredith said.

I felt completely unclean by the time I stopped the car at Fourteenth and U. I couldn't shower after practice so I was conscious of my own smell as I watched the yuppies trooping home from the Metro station. They hurried past the homeless men with their bags and shopping carts and avoided the puddles collecting in the potholes and dips at the intersection. I don't have to do this, I told myself. I don't have to sit behind those rain-streaked windows with my fingers inches away from another man's fingers and the threat of whatever hanging between us. I could still go back. I could still repackage whatever had been let loose by my telling Meredith and go home to an uncomplicated life with my Harvard early admission and two proud parents. I could go to church on Sunday and beg forgiveness for this temporary submission to wayward thoughts and for the strength to resist the ever-present temptation. No one would know. It wouldn't be cowardice. It wouldn't be running away. It would be the textbook example of taking the hard right over the easy wrong. I rummaged around the driver's side pocket. The right thing to do would have been to send a text bowing out: I'm so sorry, my car broke down. Then I could delete the app and forget the last few weeks—except that my body wouldn't let me leave. I watched the entrance to the café from across the street where a flow of young and attractive men arm in arm with women in their skinny jeans and high heels, even in this rain, streamed in and out. I should have this too, I thought.

I saw Ryan walk up the block. He was shorter than I expected, but he moved with real confidence. He bounced through each step, presumably to the rhythm of the song playing through large red headphones straddling his head. I gripped the wheel. My skin buzzed. If only whatever could happen without any impact on the rest of my life, but that's why we dream. I started the car.

Now I pass houses on Sixteenth Street that sit quietly, softly lit in the night. My parents considered living in this area when they first moved to Washington, in one of these affordable large brick homes surrounded by other black faces, near other black families with black kids also enrolled in the city's private schools. My mother would have been closer to Children's Hospital, where she has admitting privileges, and she liked the idea of a larger connected community. But my father wanted more space, and more prestige. My father likes to say that he lives in the same neighborhood as Ted Koppel. He likes the seclusion and the horse trails separating the properties. It drives me crazy because it means I have to get up that much earlier to beat slow drivers on the scenic single-lane roads. Normally it means fighting the same people who don't want to get home after work. But at this time of night, I can fly down the stretches of road between speed cameras to make up time.

My rearview mirror flashes with light from another car's high beams and then the darkness behind me pulses with red and blue lights. Shit, I yell, fuck me. There's no escaping this, not at twenty-five miles over the speed limit, after rush hour with fewer cars on the road. One of my classmates likes to brag about how he outsmarted the police after running a red light on the way home from a party over the weekend. He was going too fast for even the police to catch up and turned onto the first available side street into the first available driveway then quickly turned off his car. The police drove right by. But George Gilvert Monson Jr. has blond hair, blue eyes and a wealthy father who can afford his foolishness. I only have a wealthy father who won't subsidize mine.

I pull to the shoulder, turn on my overhead lights and place my hands on the steering wheel. Never take your hands off that wheel OJ said to me last Thanksgiving when he was stopped while driving my father's Range Rover on the way to buy extra chicken for my mother's pepper soup. Three police cars pulled into the Safeway parking lot as he tried to get into the car. They approached him with their weapons out and made him lie face-down on the wet ground while they cuffed him in front of everybody. OJ said that if our next-door neighbor hadn't walked by, he's sure that he'd have been in jail or maybe dead. But also, I kept my hands visible, he said. Always keep your hands in sight. They told him just before they left that someone had called to describe a black man trying to boost luxury cars from the village parking lot. In broad daylight, on Thanksgiving? Well you never know, the police said.

Stay calm I tell myself. Breathe easy. Breathe slow. My hands tremble as I watch a black officer approach through the rearview mirror. A white officer approaches from the passenger side. Evening son, I'm Officer Williams, I'll need to see your license and registration, the officer says. His white partner at the passenger door crosses his arms over his chest. I'm so sorry officer, I say. I know I was speeding, I'm just really late getting home. Well you might be a little bit later, he says. Your license and registration. My license is in my wallet which is in my sports bag which is in the trunk where I tossed it after practice. Your license and registration young man. I open the door and it bumps the officer. He steps backwards. The white officer raises his head, but his eyes are bored. He picks at his fingernails while looking through the passenger window. Son, what are you doing, Officer Williams says, can you please put your hands back on the wheel? I put my hands on the wheel. I'm really sorry, I say. My license is in my bag, in the trunk. Officer Green, you can step back from the vehicle please, Officer Williams says. Young man, I want you to take the keys out of your ignition and toss them out the window, can you do that for me. My keys jangle as they hit the ground. Now you can open your door from the outside, I want to see your hands. Keep them visible for me as you exit your vehicle. I push open the door with my foot and step onto the wet asphalt. The air smells of wet leaves and damp earth. I squint against the headlights of the police car. Officer Williams says, Now I'm going to hand you these keys and you can open your trunk nice and slowly for me. I pop my trunk open. My backpack sits atop a mess of empty CD cases and used towels that I meant to wash weeks ago. I reach for my bag. Can I take it out, I ask. Slowly, he says. I remove my wallet and hand my license to the officer. You can shut the trunk, he says, go back and sit in your car.

I'm not here. This isn't happening. A ticket will only add fuel to the possible fire already smoldering at home. Niru you are irresponsible. You are careless. You this boy! You don't think. Jesus! My father will shout in a tone that makes you feel like the whole world is disappointed by your birth. These are the moments when I'm almost positive that my parents never meant to have me. The perfect OJ would have been just fine for them on his own. I'd always wondered why there was such a big gap between me and OJ, that maybe I was an accident. Then my mother told me that I actually had a sister born too prematurely to survive more than a few hours after birth. That's when your father started going to church more she said. We didn't have a proper funeral. She was too young. My father has never said a word about it.

The night air is cold against my face. I should have stayed. Then Ryan and I would be on our way to doing whatever and at least being late would be worth it.

You can go now, Officer Williams says as he hands back my license through the car window. In the rearview, I see Officer Green sitting in the squad car's passenger seat. He fills the whole space with his body. Officer Williams says, listen, since you don't have any tickets or previous violations, we'll just forget that this whole thing happened. You get home now, but no more speeding, you hear? I nod but my hands won't stop shaking.

My father sits at the kitchen table waiting when I open the door. There is a place mat but no food in front of him and the space between the silver fork and knife is occupied by a small black rectangle that I know is my phone. I swallow. Good evening Daddy, I say. My father says nothing for a long time. He grinds his teeth and drums his fingers on the table. This man that usually has so much to say about everything in his deep, imposing voice and gravelly Nigerian accent is silent. I'm scared. Who is Ryan, he asks as he removes his glasses. I have not seen him like this before, angry, yes, confused, only once, but never both together. My father's hands shake as he tries to control himself. He is all power, all will. He's the one who reminds us constantly that if he could walk ten miles to get sardines and tinned tomatoes for his family during the war, dodging low-flying Nigerian fighter planes that made a sport of strafing hungry refugees, then there is nothing he or we can't do. But he can't control this.

Gwamniru, I'm asking you to tell me what is this, he shouts and his voice rises an octave with each word that leaves his mouth. His eyes narrow until they are colored only by red veins. His eyes are like that because he grew up in the dust he says, even America can't change that. When I was younger he would invert his eyelids to reveal the pink membrane beneath with its streaking capillaries. Then he would chase me from room to room laughing. I wasn't always certain that the monster behind me was really my father, so I cried. Then my father would hold me and offer me ice cream. My mother didn't like that. She says children don't like uncertainty.

Am I really seeing what my eyes are seeing, he shouts as he holds up my phone. I can make out Tinder alerts that I should have turned off. I don't know why I didn't. I can explain, I say. Explain what, he shouts and sprays a mist of saliva with the words he expels from his mouth. What will you explain? Who and who are you explaining to? My friend, keep quiet. Does your mother know about this filth you want to explain? He slams the phone down on the table. I wince. The glass vase at its center which now holds glass pens, some coins, receipts and sheets of paper that no one knows what to do with shakes and the coins inside rattle. Does your mother know? I have to tell your mother. I have to tell her that this is what her son has been doing. I never should have let your mother name you. I told her, we don't give men that kind of name, but she insisted that it had to be this name. The disgrace. I remain frozen midway between the kitchen door and the kitchen table. I want to grab the phone and break it into tiny pieces, but I can't move. Ify, my father shouts, Ify! Are you in this house? Come see what your son is doing. Are you in this house? My mother's Mercedes was in the garage when I came in, but I didn't smell any food. There is a faint odor of the trash I should have taken to the curb this morning and one of the countertops has just been sprayed with Lysol, but there is no pepper scent, no home-baked butter loaf, or any of the things she made every once in a while to remind herself that she actually could have gone to culinary school like she wanted instead of medical school like my grandfather demanded.

In my house. In this house, my father shouts. You want to bring this kind of sinful, satanic rubbish into my house. *Tufi-akwa*. It can never happen. He takes two steps toward me with the phone in his right hand before he turns around and stomps into the family room where he closes his left fist around the thorny switch of a bougainvillea twisted across the mantel. Ify, he shouts up to the landing a floor above, but my mother still doesn't answer. I told your mother, I told that woman that we should have sent you to school in Nigeria, not this useless place. How can a son of mine do this? My son? No, it can never happen. Then he charges back into the kitchen and is suddenly so close that I can smell the honey-roasted peanuts on his breath. He has only been home a few minutes and his tie still hangs from his white collar. There is a ketchup stain near the knot and I know it has probably bothered him the whole day. He is the kind of man who always wears white shirts, who cares about appearances. Before a man leaves his house each morning, he should be washed, lotioned and dressed in smart clothing. You have to pay attention to these things, he says, otherwise people will think you have no parents.

He grabs my ear. Daddy, I yelp as he twists and pulls me forward. You want to go and do gay marriage, is that what you want, you want to go and carry man, put your thing for his *nyash*? Abomination. A BOMI NATION. He pushes my face down into the kitchen table. A salty warmth fills my cheek. My tongue burns. Daddy let me tell you— Tell me what. Tell me how you want to go and collect shame and disgrace for this family. Tell me how you want to go and do all sorts of despicable, filthy, unnatural and unclean things. How can—no. You want to kill me?

The pain spreads from my cheek up to my eyes and into my forehead. My tears pool as I try to blink away the stinging feeling in my nose. I want to sneeze but I can't sneeze. I want to swallow, but I can't swallow through my constricted throat. My father lets go of me and backs away to the wall. You stupid child. You are going back to Nigeria pronto. Immediately! Sharp! Daddy you're over—I'm over what? See this boy with the audacity to open his filthy mouth and say word to me. No, you are going back to Nigeria. I will personally escort you to Holy Spirit Chapel or Mountain of Fire or whichever one so we can burn this sinful nonsense from your body. I'm overreacting—open your mouth and say it again. He launches a half-hearted slap toward me but lets his hand drop to his side. Do you know what you have done? Do you know what this means? Are you really telling me the truth, that you are going out and gallivanting with the gays, the homosexuals? Where did you learn this kind of behavior? Is it in school? Is this what are they teaching you? I'm going to call your headmaster right now. I need to speak to that your headmaster immediately, then I am buying your ticket home. We will pull you out of school and send you back to Nigeria for spiritual revival. Daddy, listen to me, I say. He straightens against the wall and his shoulder knocks the frame of one of my mother's market scene photos. It settles into a listing position. He rubs his shoulder. I'm listening, he says softly. Upstairs the toilet flushes, sending water through the pipes. My father and I look up and then at each other. I can feel my heart separate from the rest of my body. I want to hand it to the frothing old man in front of me and say, take it. It's yours, because it has always been yours, if not for your sperm, your food, and the school fees that you pay on my behalf, then who and where would I be? Nothing. I am because you are. I say nothing. Each word I search for flies from my brain before I can send it off my tongue.

Then his hands are around my neck pushing and shaking me. My ears begin to ring and I can hear myself scream even as my father's shouts grow louder in my ears. It fills my whole body with burning. His hands tighten as spittle beads on his lips. His wedding ring chafes my skin and I wish it would sever something that can end this immediately. If there is anything like a bright spot it's imagining what he will do when that first spurt of blood erupts from my throat and spatters on the ceiling. But maybe he will smile at having done the Lord's work to rid the world of such abominable evil. Maybe he will cite the story of Abraham and Isaac from whatever damp cinder-block prison enclosure the state would carve out for him. I hold his collar in my hands. His sweat has made the material soft. I pull and my father's head snaps back. Speak, *ngwa*. You said you want to talk then talk. Tell me with that your filthy mouth. Let me hear what you want to say. My father bangs my head against the wall and the room vibrates. He slaps me once and then again. Speak you bloody fool.

Obi, stop, stop it, *kwusi*. Are you trying to kill my son, you want me to lose another child, my mother shouts, *mba, mba, mba.* I can see her now in her purple housecoat and shower cap. I can smell the rose-scented milk bar that she uses, that she buys in multiple packs because I steal them from her. Her face is wet, from the shower, from tears, I can't tell. She forces herself between us, pushes Dad back with both hands and encircles me in the smell of roses and damp terry cloth. Obi, have you lost your mind, she says as she touches my face. What in the name of ever-loving God are you doing to my child? Ask him, my father shouts, ask that thing what I'm doing to him. I'm sending you back to Nigeria, no more of this rubbish, no more. I will clean you up. I will clean you— Obi, *chelu,* my mother says as she holds me up. The room spins around me. My mother touches my head and I feel like fainting. Calm down, can't you see he's bleeding, she says. How can I be calm? This is not a matter of calm. There is no calm here. My father moves towards us. I shrink into the wall. It's enough, it's enough, she shouts. You want me to call police for you? She is crying. Look at me. Can you see me? Goddammit, she says. She never says that. *Chineke,* she wails. I collapse into her shoulder and sink down as my knees give and the air rushes back into my chest between sobs. My brain searches for something like strength or dignity, but the space before my eyes is blank and empty, except for this pain. So you think it's okay that your son wants to run around with the gays, my father shouts, you want him to follow them and marry man. My mother's arms stiffen beneath my shoulders. She looks down at me, then she looks away.

34

3

My mother wakes me up by turning on the lights. My eyes burn and my head throbs. She opens the door quietly, but I know she has been standing there for some time. Her shadow sweeps across my bedroom floor. She has tried her best not to hover since what I've come to think of as "The Great Revealing" but I feel her worry as intensely as I feel my father's disgust. I hear her dart halfway up the stairs with each loud noise I make in my bedroom. I watch her feet shift outside my door while she tries to decide if she should knock or just leave me be. The night it all happened, she helped me from the kitchen up to my bathroom and said nothing until after she pulled the first aid kit from underneath the cabinet, placed it on the bathtub lip beside her and used a warm wet gauze to clean the cut that opened when my father banged my head against the wall. It will be okay she whispered as she held me and rubbed away the dried blood on the back of my neck. She smeared Neosporin on my cuts and kissed my forehead.

I know why she hovers. It was only a few years ago that OJ and I came home from school to find my mother's car nudged up against the garage wall, with the doors open, the key in the ignition, engine running, the gear in drive. OJ's hands shook as he reached into the car, placed the gear in park and retrieved the keys. He told me to wait while he crept up the steps. The kitchen door was wide open and her flats lay scattered haphazardly on the floor by the kitchen table. Maybe we should call 911, I said. I had ignored his instruction to stay in the garage because it seemed safer not to be alone waiting for whoever or whatever had done this to come back. OJ handed me his phone and said, get ready, as we moved slowly through the kitchen. We found my mother in the powder room splashing water on her face. If she was surprised to see us, it didn't show. She asked OJ to get the ibuprofen from her handbag. She followed us from the powder room to the kitchen still holding a pink hand towel. She pulled us both close and then broke into sobs. A patient in her care for the last ten years had committed suicide. Her parents found her in her bedroom with an empty bottle of whiskey and prescription sleeping pills. She was seventeen.

That night I told my mother, I'm not going to kill myself, but I spoke as much to my reflection as to her. It was the first thing I'd said since we left the kitchen. I know, she said but she still sat at my desk after she switched off my bedroom lights. The chair creaked every time she nodded off.

The days since then have been a timeless fuzz. I feel time pass but nothing actually seems to happen. I've heard my parents argue on the landing. The boy should go to school, I hear my father say, enough of this nonsense, it's because you have treated him like a woman that he's behaving like this, he should get up and get ready. Are you really that phenomenally stupid, I hear my mother say. She speaks softly but my father shouts in a voice he knows I will hear. You want him to go to school looking like this because you can't control your anger? I had a very good reason. You think these people don't take note of things like that. Let them take note. They can mark the progress because I'm not even close to being finished. If you touch my son again, I will kill you myself. Do you hear me? Let them bring police, FBI, CIA, whichever one, but I will kill you myself. Have all your senses just left you? He's your son for God's sake. Your own son. I don't care. Then get out of this house. What? I said you will get out of this house, just get out of my sight until you're prepared to sound like a reasonable human being. Ify? Get. Out.

Sometimes I wonder how my parents found each other. They are so different, like matter and antimatter, and I don't know that their marriage won't zap itself into oblivion. My mother comes from a family that has always had everything. She was born during the civil war years, in Kenya where my grandfather worked as a doctor with the World Health Organization. Her brothers live in places like South Kensington and Sandton where they run banks and mobile phone companies. One of her sisters is a geologist who fell in love with an Australian while completing her masters at

Cambridge. She lives in Perth with twin girls whose lean figures, sand-colored hair and blue eyes already have them modeling. Her youngest sister stayed in Nigeria and married a civil servant who owns a lot of real estate in the capital. My mother went to medical school but learned French because my grandfather liked to read Rimbaud and Baudelaire. My grandmother was a teacher and filled their homes with books and paintings.

My father is a true village boy from eastern Nigeria who lived a childhood of near starvation, neglect and an everyday struggle against enemies trying to crush him at every turn. He went to University of Nsukka, graduated first in his class and then got an oil company scholarship to do his graduate degree in America. My parents met during National Youth Service after he came back to Nigeria with an MBA from Columbia University. My mother says she fell in love with him because he knew exactly where he was going, but his strong sense of direction sometimes presents its own set of problems.

I'm not coming out, I say into my pillow. I have left my bed only to use the toilet and after even those short steps I've felt weak and exposed. I can smell myself in my sheets. I am on the verge of smelling like the homeless men and women in McPherson Square and at Union Station. Niru, love, we're going to church, my mother says. She sits on the bed beside me and strokes my cheek with the back of her fingers. Can you please get up and get ready? It's important.

Her voice sounds gravelly and that makes me turn to her. She's already dressed in blue pants and a white top with a yellow cardigan but she hasn't done her makeup. I push her hand away from my face. My stomach growls. Will Daddy be there, I ask. I don't know, she says, I haven't really spoken with your father. But that's not the point. If he's there or if he's not there, we should still go. Sometimes it's good to put your problems before God. She gets up and draws back my curtains, allowing a gray light to sweep into the room. My eyes slowly adjust to the new light. I can see outside to the driveway covered in a wet shine from the previous night's rain. The garbage and recycling bins still sit at the top of the driveway. She says, he's your father, Niru, you will have to talk with him at some point. I'll be waiting for you in the kitchen. At the doorway she pauses and holds on to the frame. How's your head, she asks. I touch my scalp. I tell her my head still hurts.

The idea of church doesn't appeal to me. Not that I don't believe—I do, I think—but since sophomore year, Sunday morning services have become inconvenient. Sometimes there's homework, sometimes there's sleep. I was baptized in that church and we've been going ever since the beginning when Reverend Olumide decided that the old banking hall on Sixteenth Street would become his new temple because God had seen fit to give a young Nigerian preacher the vision and fortitude to turn this space into a bastion of the Word. Reverend Olumide and my father have known each other since before they came to the States in the eighties. My father went to New York and Reverend Olumide went to Texas. They were reunited by chance in Washington, D.C. Reverend Olumide has a daughter OJ's age, an actress in Los Angeles but she grew up with her mom in Oakland,

California. That's why you don't marry these white girls, my father always says to OJ, they don't have staying power, they will take your children and then your kids end up all over the place. It's probably better that the Reverend isn't married, or maybe it's why he isn't married anymore, because all his energy goes into the church. The photos from when I was baptized show my mother carrying me in all white, standing with OJ and my father before two massive, peeling wood entrance doors. There were large dust-covered windows with cracked panes on either side and chipped concrete lions at the top of the steps. It's different now. The front windows are two stories of stained-glass crosses that cast rainbow colors onto manicured grass and shrubs, and the large entry doors have been replaced with carved mahogany from Nigeria. There's a white marble slab above them that says ALL ARE WELCOME. The basement used to be a maze of concrete walls and exposed pipes that we would run through while our parents tried to focus on gospels and sermons in the sanctuary above. Now it has brightly lit, carpeted spaces with rooms for day care and community group meetings. There's a library and a music room. It sometimes seems that every African living in the D.C. area goes to this church, Nigerians, Ghanians, Cameroonians, Congolese. Some work for embassies. Some are taxi drivers. Some are illegal, but they are all truly welcome. Reverend Olumide has even learned Spanish and now holds a smaller service in the afternoons for the Salvadorians and Guatemalans in search of something less exclusionary than Catholicism. We must grow or perish, he says at the pulpit from time to time.

Church is always packed on Sundays. This Sunday is no different. I look around the sanctuary at pews jammed into the space between rows of concrete pillars. They are full of dark-skinned faces turned up towards the reverend and his Plexiglas lectern. Reverend Olumide paces across the dais and dabs his forehead with a soiled white handkerchief. He hardly needs a microphone, but his sermons are recorded for his podcast so we suffer the fuzzy distortion that fills the room when he gets animated. I sit behind my mother and reach for a Bible and hymnal. I can sneak at least fifteen minutes of napping if I keep a Bible open on my lap and put my chin to my chest. My father hates this, but he isn't here.

You'll never guess what the kingdom of God has in store for you, Reverend Olumide shouts. You can never imagine what awaits you when you open that door and embrace fully the light of life. "But Reverend, Pastor, how do I open that door," some of you will ask me. "You say if I believe then all will be revealed." My brothers and my sisters, declaring Jesus Christ of Nazareth as your Lord and Savior is just one step of a continuous and life-long process. Listen to me very well now cause what I'm about to say is really important. Yes sir, the congregation mumbles. I'm not going to tell you something that you aren't trying to hear, that's me wasting my breath, Reverend Olumide says. So do you want to know? Yes, tell us, the congregation shouts. My mother shouts too. If you want to know say Amen. Amen! If you want to know, say Hallelujah. Hallelujah, Jesus is Lord! Reverend Olumide stops behind his lectern. His hands circle the microphone and he exhales loudly. My brothers and my sisters, I want to tell you that I am a sinner. The congregation gasps. I am a sinner and I'm probably going to sin again. Lord forgive me. I have sinned against Jesus in my actions and my thoughts. Every day I sin, I sin like a champion. You know how Michael Phelps won the Olympic gold for swimming. Well I would have won the Olympics in sinning. Everybody laughs. So does my mother even if she shakes her head. But even with that, even with my championship ways, my Lord and Savior Jesus has seen fit to show me the key to God's kingdom. Can I get an Amen? The older women clutch the pews. A young mother cradles her baby in one arm and the Bible in the other. Repentance, my brothers and my sisters, repentance is the key, Reverend Olumide shouts. Amen. Look yourself in the eye, acknowledge that you are a champion sinner, and then with all of your heart and humility tell Jesus that you are unworthy but you beg His pardon. Say it with me, repentance is the key. Repentance is the key, they shout. One more time now, repentance is the key. Repentance is the key. I mumble to myself, repentance is not for me, before I stand up and slink out from the pew towards the entrance. My mother turns to look at me, her mouth open. I catch her eye, lower my head and step outside.

The clouds nuzzle up against one another in a bright blue sky while the sun struggles to warm everything below. I sit down on the steps that push their cold through my corduroy slacks and I pull my blazer tighter around my chest. The street stretches into the distance in either direction, its silence occasionally interrupted by a jogger puffing heavily behind condensing breath. I should have run this weekend, especially since Coach Erickson pulled me aside after the first practice to give me a lengthy speech about the possibilities for the season. You have potential, real potential, he said as his hands stroked the salt and pepper of his smartly groomed beard. Meredith watched us from across the field. That's how we're going to run you and how we're going to train you, I think you've got a conference championship and record if you want it. He paused for a moment to scratch beneath the waves of dark brown hair that flow down his neck. He finished college as a distance runner with Olympic prospects, getting as far as the trials for the fifteen hundred meters in Athens. He knew how to run, but he also knew what makes molecules stick together. He taught Honors Chemistry and liked to take what he called a scientific approach to running. That meant practice, practice and more practice. Ten thousand hours Niru, he said to me. You ready?

I know I am supposed to want it. So much of me does want it, does want to have something that's entirely mine, that OJ for all his effort and charm can't have. He was a middling sprinter at best, even if he was still a team captain. This is supposed to be my season to carve my own space if I play my cards right. That means focus, Saturday conditioning, Sunday conditioning. Meredith and I have drawn up a schedule and this weekend was supposed to be our five-mile run on the gravel paths beneath the bare oak and maple branches along the C&O Canal, but it didn't happen—for obvious reasons—and that has jeopardized every- thing. Do I want it? I want so many things, so many competing things. I want to run to win, to run away from myself, to run away from home. That would break my mother. She still keeps a tiny picture of my sister in her wallet. I know because I saw it once when she emptied her handbag on the table as she searched for her car keys. She quickly snatched it up from under a pile of credit cards and lipstick tubes when my hand reached towards it. I've heard her say, it can't happen to me again, when she stands outside my room. Lightning cannot strike twice.

Aren't you cold, my mother asks. Her shadow falls across my body and I shiver. You should have brought your jacket. You boys. If someone doesn't remind you, you'd forget to wear your clothes. Then she sits down beside me. She folds her hands in her lap and breathes in deeply each time she wants to say something. She does this with contractors and delivery people, anyone she feels might not listen—a deep breath in, her eyes closed, and then her words coming out on the next breath before she can think again. She says, I remember when we brought you for your baptism. I look at her. The sunlight flickers on her face as fast-moving clouds slide across the sky. You wouldn't stop crying, you kept fussing in your little white *agbada*. I tried to feed you but you wouldn't eat, you wouldn't take the pacifier, you wouldn't even suck your own thumb. I was worried that you'd disturb the whole service. It was embarrassing. You this boy can really make noise. Your father, he was worried too. That I'd already rejected Jesus Christ as my Lord and Savior? My mother places her hand on the back of my neck. Her fingers are cold. He was afraid that you'd gotten sick on the way from the car to the church. He was blaming himself for not dressing you up properly, he felt so bad.

I hug my arms tighter across my chest. Your father should be here any moment now, she says. I look up. I thought it would be best if we all talked with Reverend Olumide, as a family. You didn't tell me, I say. I stand up but she grabs my hand and pulls me back down to the steps. I try to stand again but she won't let go. She loops her arm in mine and slides closer. I told you I didn't know he was coming, and I didn't know, he just texted me now. You said you hadn't spoken to him. You people treat me like I'm stupid. Watch yourself young man, I can only take so much of this. For the last few days I've said nothing, just tried to make sure you're okay, but do you consider if I'm okay? Do you think I even know what to think? Every day I pray, I pray to God to keep you and your brother safe, to keep your father safe and then this happens. I don't even know what to think. My son, have some pity for your mother *abeg*. Me, I'm trying okay. I'm really really trying for you. But you have to help me, *biko*, you have to help us. The door opens behind us and the sound of the congregation singing the closing hymn spills out into the street. My mother and I stand up and separate before we turn around. Reverend Olumide stands in his suit with his Lenten purple stole flapping in the breeze.

Ify, Niru, he says, with a quick nod. Obi is here now. He's in my office. You can come up when you're ready. He steps back and the door shuts. My mother steps forward and then slips inside. I won't force you Niru, she says, but please.

—————

Obi please, can you just take a deep breath and sit down, Reverend Olumide says, pointing at the armchair on the opposite side of the coffee table. His office is large with windows overlooking Sixteenth Street and the park beyond it. I have only been inside a few times before, but this space has also changed over the years, growing more lavish with upgraded furniture, a massive glass and chrome table, modern chrome-frame armchairs and a long puffy leather couch that squeaks when we sit down. The walls behind his desk are plastered with books from floor to ceiling, each section carefully labeled according to some particular aspect of faith or theology. Reverend Olumide meets once with each confirmation class in his office for pizza, sodas and a discussion about the importance of faith. Then he meets each student individually before Confirmation Sunday just to make sure we're ready. That's how I know times are better now than they were five years ago when I was confirmed. Five years ago his furniture looked like it came from a garage sale.

Reverend Olumide perches at the edge of his desk while my mother and I sit on the couch and my father continues to pace. This is not about judgment, Reverend Olumide says—we know exactly what the scripture says—this is about a path toward forgiveness. My mother moves to the edge of the couch and places her hands in her lap. My father's feet pound the floor with each step. The Bible says, Reverend Olumide begins—I'm not interested in what the Bible says Paul, my father snaps. I'm interested in what we are doing to undo this psychological and spiritual corruption in my son's brain. That's what I want to know. Can the Bible tell me that? Obi, my mother says. Her jaw clenches. I'm serious Ify, I didn't come here to pontificate on scripture. I came to save my son. Reverend Olumide says, it's through scripture that your son will be saved. Remember we leave to the Lord what the Lord alone can fix. This is not a man-made thing. His salvation is something of the spirit and to deal with spiritual things we need a combined psychological and spiritual approach. I have reached out to my close friend who has real experience with disturbances of this nature and he has agreed to help.

What if I don't need help, I say. Excuse me, my father says. My mother shifts closer to me and Reverend Olumide steps forward from his desk. Obi, for God's sake sit down, he says, but my father ignores him. Reverend Olumide sits down in the chair facing me. Young man, what do you mean by this, this is a serious thing to say, we all need to be saved. Reverend Olumide holds a deep furrow between his eyebrows. He puckers his lips up to his nostrils as if struck by a terrible smell. Niru, this is a very serious matter you know, your parents, myself, we are all here because we are concerned. Well maybe you shouldn't be. Maybe you should just let me be. I've done everything right. I get good grades. I come to church, I believe in God, I'm going to Harvard. You make it seem like it would be better if I murdered someone. Maybe it would, my father says. What is your problem, I say as I stand up. Easy my friend. Easy, Reverend Olumide says, this is your father. You are talking to your father. We don't speak like that to our elders no matter what. This is not our way. My father says, you see what this place is doing to this boy. Well what does he want me to do then.

I can commit murder. It's not that hard, I say, staring directly at my father.

My father won't look at me, but I can see his scowl growing. My mother searches her bag for a tissue. Her loose change clinks as her handbag shakes on her knees. You people are losing focus here, she says. Reverend, please, we've discussed this. Discussed what, I ask. I look at each person in the room. And nobody asked me? Niru, can you please take your seat, Reverend Olumide says. My father says, nobody asked you because you're still a child and you don't know what you are doing to your life. I'm not a child. I'm eighteen. This is my life. You clearly don't have the judgment to make the right decisions. This is not a decision, I shout. So I am making them for you, as your father, under the guidance of the pastor here. My father slaps an open palm against his chest as he stares me down. My brothers, can we both just take our seats, Reverend Olumide shouts. I'm perfectly capable of deciding for myself. You can't do anything without me, my father says. Just look at this mess you've gotten us into now. Look at the shame on us now because you are deciding for yourself. Enough is enough already. I've had enough of your foolishness for one morning. Reverend Olumide shouts, everyone sit down. My father says, there is a time for niceties and there is a time we just have to be responsible as parents, and that's just it. All this talk is just a waste of precious air. Your mother and I talked to Reverend here and we are taking you home for some serious spiritual counseling and deliverance. Reverend has already recommended us someone who can clear this abomination from you.

I sink backwards to the couch. I look at my mother who seems so small now, like she wants to hide behind her crumpled tissue or slip into the cracks between the leather cushions. Mommy, you're part of this? She says, it's for your own good, Niru. Then she is quiet. Reverend Olumide places both his hands into his pockets and rocks back and forth from his heels to his toes. The street below is awake now and buzzes with families headed to the park. The clouds above have slowed their pace and cluster in large patches, blocking the sun and casting darkness over the room. I blink.

4

The airplane rumbles to a full stop, shaking the luggage in the bins overhead and the seat backs in front. I watch my father relax his grip on the armrest, cross himself and mutter a silent prayer of thanks before he opens his eyes to cast sideways glances at the passengers already standing in the aisle. See our people, my father says, but I press my forehead against the window and look out at the carcasses of scrapped airplanes rusting in the tall grass by the tarmac. The terminal looms into view with its powerful lights trained on airplanes waiting to unload passengers and cargo before quickly loading up again for return journeys to America, Europe, and the Middle East, maybe even China. I watch men and women in reflective yellow jackets scramble around the luggage crates and large-wheeled utility trucks and tugs. I'm too far away to see the sweat on their faces, but I can feel the heat and humidity already. My father inhales deeply as he struggles to remove his sweater and roll up his shirtsleeves. He checks for his passport and asks me to double-check for mine. The thin green book sits safely in the backpack pocket that should hold my smart-phone. But I don't have a smart-phone anymore. I pull it out and hand it to him. He caresses the cover and then slips it into his shirt pocket. When the seatbelt sign blinks off, he springs up from his seat. Come on, he says, be fast now, let's go.

My father becomes an entirely different man when we come to Nigeria. OJ came up with a term for the condition during a trip we took the summer after his first year in medical school. He said Daddy had a bad case of Nigeriatoma, an acute swelling of ego and pride that affects diaspora Nigerian men, rendering them unable to accept the idea that a true home might exist outside of their birth country. Symptoms may vary but are exceptionally pronounced upon return to native soil and include hyperactivity, elevated mood, grandiose thinking and increased aggression. The differential includes bipolar disorder and indeed those afflicted have much in common with patients observed in the thrall of a manic episode. The duration of symptoms may vary, but poor electricity, bad roads and exposure to extreme heat have proven effective as treatment. My mother laughed at that, my father too, but only because OJ said it.

My father's transformation is swift. His chest puffs out and his arms swing into action. He forces his way through the airport meeting each official who dares to slow his entry into the promised land with a "try me" stare-down and where appropriate, a cajoling mix of pidgin and Igbo. He seems taller as he leans toward these officials, forcing them to shrink back in the face of his momentum. Mr. Jacob, the driver my father always uses when he comes home, stands waiting for us by his black Toyota Camry when we finally step out from the arrivals terminal into the shouting mass of men with dust-reddened, irritated and sleep-deprived eyes, each asking if we need a taxi. It is hot and there is a vague smell of decay and burning as if the whole world smolders. It surrounds me and seeps into me. I blink at these figures in long-sleeve shirts unbuttoned at the collar, with their dress slacks or jeans and wonder how they can possibly survive wearing such heavy clothes. They have wet patches beneath their arms. They wipe their faces with handkerchiefs every other minute. Looking at them makes me feel hot and tired.

I've always felt weird about coming to Nigeria. Everything is always so overwhelming and aggressive from the moment we step out of the airport and into a country that my father loves so deeply he had to run away from it. But I've never had a choice. No one has ever asked me. Each summer my father's momentum dragged us all home. His excitement sent my mother to the big-box stores to buy clothes, shoes and handbags to distribute to the aunties and uncles in the village. In the weeks leading up to each trip, he grew restless and wondered why OJ and I didn't share his level of enthusiasm. OJ was smart enough to keep his mouth shut and nod when my father said, come on boys, show some excitement, we're going home. I never learned. But this is home, I said once as we sat at the kitchen table. No it's not, my father snapped, this place is not your home not now, not ever. He speared a piece of beef with his fork and then let the utensil clatter against the plate. I stared across the table into my father's eyes searching for some recognition that here in Washington, we had our own house full of our things, pictures of us as a family, books collected over the years, my toys, random trinkets. Here my parents drove their own cars and always knew where they were going. We had our church, and they had jobs they went to every single day. On some days the word Nigeria never even leaves your mouth, I wanted to shout. My father's face gave nothing. He said, Nigeria is home.

But no matter how many times we came "home," everything was so uncomfortable for me. My father never seemed to notice that his shirt stuck to his back with sweat, or if he noticed he didn't care. I hated the fact that everyone walked around in a cloud of body odor so thick it almost formed a visible aura around them. I hated the discomfort sitting in traffic, discomfort sitting in the darkness when the power went out—it was always going out—the constant vibration of the generators and their exhaust fumes. I hated the forever-uneasy feeling in my stomach after each meal that sent me to bathrooms that however spotless always carried a whiff of sewage. This was not home, not to me even if I secretly loved the thunderstorms and the smell of wet red earth after the rains. I wanted to ask how I should really feel about streets packed with potholes and gutters full to the brim with trash and sludge. I wanted to know how to relax when the cars beside you drove so close that you could see the red veins in the drivers' eyes because everyone treated the lane dividers as suggestions. It was almost too confusing to see the old and decrepit so close to the new and shiny, the jalopies held together by string and prayer next to brand-new Mercedes SUVs, the straw, palm leaf and plywood squatter settlements next to white walls protecting the large sparkling glass windows of unreasonably sized mansions that would have looked more comfortable in Hollywood. And everywhere there were people, some going places, some unmoving and happy to let the world happen around them, but covering every free space with a visible sense of entitlement no matter how tattered or well-kept their clothing. I had the irrational fear that I would disappear into the mess of all these people and never be seen or heard from again.

For chrissake, Niru, OJ would say to me, get over yourself. Your sulking is making everybody miserable. There's so much here. But OJ liked to go visiting with my father and sit on the verandas of old houses to listen to old men tell stories in Igbo about the old days while the crickets and the frogs croaked and chirped in the background. I couldn't understand.

You don't have to go, he can't make you go, that's like abduction, Meredith said when I told her my father was taking me to Nigeria. She said, shit I can't believe he hit you, like he beat you up, and she examined my face. My lips were still swollen and there was a cut on my cheek that had only started to heal. I told people I fell off my bike and we all laughed at my being an idiot. He didn't beat me up, we just got into a fight, it happens, I said before I half sprinted down the straightaway towards the cluster of teammates stretching half-heartedly at the opposite end. The girls' track team wore black sweats and we wore blue. The two colors remained relatively separate except for the odd pair of upperclassmen chatting while we stretched. Tell him you have track practice, Meredith said when she caught up. She put her hand on my shoulder to balance while she stretched her quads. I did, I said. Her eyes locked with mine as she caught her breath. He asked me if it was impossible to run in Nigeria, then he asked me if Nigeria sent runners to the Olympics, or was he dreaming, I said. Then come stay with me, she said, you can come live at my house until we go to college. Don't they kill gay people in Nigeria, she whispered. Her hand clutched my shoulder harder. They don't kill people, it's just fourteen years in prison, I said. Niru what the fuck—no you can't go, like you just can't go. If you go you're never coming back. Her eyes shot back and forth across my face. You don't even seem to give a shit. Of course I do, I just can't do anything about it, I said. You can come live with me, she pleaded. I thought about it only because it would cause my father a fair amount of pain. I imagined him lowering his head when people asked, what happened to that your son, the younger one? But it was never an option. The thought of perpetual self-consciousness, of walking from an unfamiliar bedroom to an unfamiliar bathroom in the mornings, of eating salmon and steak tartare instead of jollof rice and egusi soup with *okporopo*—even though I don't like really *okporopo*—didn't feel like home either. Your house is too cold, I told Meredith. I'm serious Niru, she said loud enough for everyone around us to look up, this is crazy.

I have no desire to be here, but I also know there are battles that you fight to fight and battles that you fight to win, and refusing to get on the plane was not going to do anyone any good.

Now I am here and there is no going back. My father holds my passport and the tickets. I am under his control. The world around me feels out of alignment like a globe rattling and wobbling on its stand as it spins. As we leave the terminal, I can see where I'm going but with every step the ground shifts just a little and my sense of direction becomes confused. I wonder if my father and Reverend Olumide are right, maybe there is something truly abominable about me that only the purifying fire of constant prayer can purge. Maybe I have spent too much time in the United States soaking up ungodly values and satanic sentiments, as my father has said, and that has created a confusion only the motherland can cure. Or maybe I'm just me. It seems unlikely that this prescribed week with prayer warriors will make a difference but Reverend Olumide says it's just the start. He says there are acute and chronic interventions. When I return I'm supposed to meet with him weekly. Maybe that's not a bad thing.

Mr. Jacob smiles his gap-toothed smile when he sees me. He has transformed from a youngish man with a full head of hair to a middle-aged man with a scraped head to mask his early baldness. I hustle towards the car and Mr. Jacob's outstretched hand. *Oga*, he says to my father, look at this small pickin, so big now. Wondaful! God has truly bless you! My father says nothing. Mr. Jacob says to me, ah ah, look at how much you have changed. When we finally settle into the backseat of Mr. Jacob's car, my father gives a two-hundred-Naira note to the police officer waiting expectantly. Okay Jacob, let's go, he says.

We stay in the guest chalet at Aunty Amara's house. It's a small but tastefully decorated two-bedroom bungalow across a courtyard from the main house. There is an empty swimming pool between. My mother says Aunty Amara was always the most beautiful of the three girls from the day she was born and that she's used that beauty to her advantage. She married Uncle Victor, a wealthy civil servant turned businessman fifteen years older than her who always has money but never seems to work. My father hates Uncle Victor. He calls him, "one of those," which is his way of describing someone so steeped in "the corruption" that he has no sense of right and wrong.

My father wakes me the next morning just as I conquer my jet lag and find an uneasy sleep. He stands in the doorway wearing the clothes he traveled in, his white shirt wrinkled and his trousers full of creases. His belt is undone. He holds his glasses loosely between his thumb and index finger as he massages his eyes with his free hand. He looks uncertain and badly in need of sleep but my mother isn't around to check his more manic tendencies. Mr. Jacob is already here, we need to get ready quickly so we can make it to the village on time, my father says before he turns around and crosses the corridor to his bedroom. The call to prayer sounds in the distance as lizards scratch around the roof. I swing my feet to the floor and my toes curl against the cold granite tiles. The early morning departure from Aunty Amara's house is another ritual for my father. He hates staying here despite its convenience and the luxury. Outside, the main house looms above the guest chalet, its white paint sparkling with the rising sun. My mother, OJ, and I always wanted to stay here longer because of the swimming pool and the army of white-uniformed house staff who set a fully prepared breakfast out on the dining table in the mornings. My mother likes to tease Aunty Amara that of all the girls she married the best. Uncle Victor owns a bank and houses across Nigeria, in London and South Africa. Her twins go to boarding school in Switzerland and Uncle Victor has a private jet. My father hates staying here because he hates depending on people—especially in his own country, on a man his own age, but mostly I think he's jealous. Sometimes he tells my mother, if I had stayed don't you think we would have had all this. She says, if you stayed you wouldn't have had me. I don't know that my father always considers that a fair trade. Appearances matter to him. That's why we live in Avenel instead of Prince George's County. That's why he drives a Range Rover and wears a Rolex with his tailored suits and Ferragamos. You have to pay attention to these things, my father says, don't give the world any reason to doubt you. A gay son, what would the world think of that?

I slip into my clothes and splash water on my face in the bathroom. When I step out onto the small patio, Mr. Jacob is already hard at work with a rag in one hand and the garden hose in the other spraying and wiping as he makes a circular orbit around a late-model Prado parked in the shadow of the main house. I can see the muscles in his bare back tense and relax as he strains to make the vehicle shine. If you can do nothing else, at least look decent, my father likes to say. He also says, there is no decency in Nigeria. Mr. Jacob looks at me from across the hood and smiles. The last few years have not treated him kindly and his worries, his younger brother, his kids, his wife, all of whom cost money, are etched on his face. *Oga* Niru, I dey greet you, he says, waving an arc of water across the car hood. Na long journey for today, but we thank God. I wave back and drag my carry-on to the car. When we were younger, we would pile all the bags full of gifts in the back, squeeze our suitcases beside them and then huddle together, my mother on one side, OJ on the other, me sandwiched in the middle with my legs straddling the floor hump. If I fell asleep on OJ, he jerked an elbow to push me off. My mother let me snuggle into her shoulder, the one bit of comfort she received on a journey she hated. If my mother had her way, we would make the trip by plane—forty-five minutes instead of seven hours—but my father hates flying, especially in Nigeria. It makes his blood pressure skyrocket. He hides it with his claims that he wants me and OJ to get to know our country and what better way to do that than to watch as clear skies over open plains of brown scrub and mudbrick, thatched-roof huts give way to green hills dotted with cement houses and tin roofs beneath the large gray clouds. Each year, OJ and I have watched it all pass in an air-conditioned SUV from which my father always points out the dwarf goats crossing the road and the straw-hatted Fulani herdsmen shuffling behind emaciated cows they hope to sell in the south. You could be them, OJ says. My mother says, I forbid it in Jesus Name. I say, but I'm not.

My father appears on the patio in a fresh shirt and chinos with his jacket draped over his carry-on. Did you take your bath, he asks loud enough for Mr. Jacob to hear. I ignore the question as I contemplate whether to honor duty and take his bag to the car, but Mr. Jacob leaps forward and grabs the suitcase from my father's hand. *Oga sah*, good morning, he says and stomps his foot. Good morning O, my father says back. How can you be carrying my bag when we have this young man here to help us, he says as he stares at me. Mr. Jacob yanks the bag from my father's loose grip. I inhale and feel the air burn my nostrils and throat. I feel like I don't exhale until we reach my grandfather's house in the village.

I never met my grandfather. He died two years before I was born, and my father never says much about him except that he died drunk and broke, leaving nothing for the family except his small bungalow squatting beneath two mango trees that have never produced any fruit but at least provide shade for the cinder-block walls that would otherwise absorb the intense sun. My grandfather never managed to paint the house, not even when my father sent money, so its gray walls and steel burglary bars in the windows make it feel like a prison. At the far end of the small compound near the wall is my grandfather's grave. It lies beneath a scraggly orange tree. When my father dies he will be buried there. When I die I am supposed to be buried there too. My father hates this house because it is crude and simple, especially compared to the larger modern structures that now line the unpaved roads in the village. Still he makes us come every year because home is home, even if you have to bathe from buckets and eat food cooked over an open charcoal flame. My mother hates it but she says nothing except, your father has his reasons.

Our arrival sparks the interests of a few village boys who cluster at the compound gates to watch Mr. Jacob wipe down the car. My father struggles with the front door until brute force twists the key in the padlock on the grate, the lock opens and the door swings outward on its hinges. A block of sunlight settles into the dark dusty room. Within moments he has circled the small parlor and thrown open all the windows so that the sunlight illuminates the burgundy-colored furniture. The room smells of a thick dust that settles on my tongue and makes me cough. Mr. Jacob, can you call those boys, my father shouts through an open window. He louvers the glass slats up and down and then runs a finger over the thick layer of gray dust settled on the surface. *Biko* tell them I have work for them to do.

There should be an older woman, Mama Chikwu, who opens the house for us weeks before we arrive, but her husband died last Christmas and she left to join her daughter and grandson in Lagos. She swept the veranda and kept the weeds that clustered around the foundation at bay. She exorcised the house of cockroaches and lizard droppings. She doused the bathrooms with Dettol and captured rain water. She would have arranged for someone else to tidy up the house, but this visit my father didn't call ahead. He flops onto the sofa, raising a cloud of dust that catches in the afternoon sunlight. Here we are, home, he says with his arms spread wide.

Oga sah, they are ready, Mr. Jacob says through the open slats. He holds his hands out to a group of preteen boys with spindly legs and arms sticking out from their ragtag shorts and T-shirts. We have only a few childhood pictures of my father, but his younger self looked just like them. I have two thousand Naira for each of you if you're ready to work this afternoon, my father says in Igbo. I need people to cut this grass, sweep, fetch water and wash these windows. The boys whisper excitedly at the prospect of two thousand Naira for work they do every day for free. My father looks at me as if to say, see what I spared you.

I join them because it feels wrong to stand around while boys younger than me work to clean the house I will be living in, but also because I have no desire to follow my father as he makes his first stops to let the necessary distant relatives and old friends know that we have arrived. OJ calls them "the extras" because they remind him of the people used as background in movies about white people in Africa. There are the old men who grip your shoulder and demand you call them Uncle after telling the same old story in a disjointed mixture of Igbo and English of how in primary school, they conspired with my father to steal the head teacher's chickens. My father gives them all tall bottles of Johnnie Walker Black and sheepishly distributes crumpled Naira notes for their memories. It beats standing awkwardly in front of round-bodied women in multicolored cloth who call me fine boy even while they scold me for not speaking Igbo. They say, you must learn to speak it now, it is your language, this is your home. OJ speaks Igbo—badly—but everybody loves him because at least he tries. My father loves to show him off. They walk these red-earth roads from house to house so he can say this is my boy, my first son, the one I told you is studying to become a medical doctor, a surgeon at Columbia University. I see my father slip out with Mr. Jacob. He doesn't even ask me to come.

The boys are embarrassed for me and try to stop me from taking a grungy rag soaked in soapy water to the windows. They attack the cracking cement floor on their hands and knees to rub away spots of obvious grime from the parlor. I move to the bedrooms with a rag and bucket. Mr. Jacob has placed our carry-ons in my grandfather's bedroom just at the foot of his large and unsteady bed. Yellowed mosquito netting hangs limply from its four posts. The sheets are still crisply folded but covered in dust and lizard droppings. I use the broom to sweep the dry pellets to the floor. My father will sleep here surrounded by the belongings of a man he equally loved and despised. Aside from pictures of a wiry little man who covered his bald head with a tattered trucker's hat, I have no sense of what my grandfather was like. My father says he never spoke much and he drank a lot after my grandmother was killed during the war. Some people just can't take the trauma, my father told me and OJ when we flipped through an old photo album at home. He didn't sound angry, but I could hear that he considered my grandfather weak.

I wipe down the wooden bedframe and then turn my attention to the glass-fronted cabinet on the wall facing the bed. It has not been touched in years and holds a multicolored collection of cups set upside down on their rims. I wipe the dust-caked shelves with my rag but only succeed in smearing gray streaks across the greenish glass. Behind the cups are miniature bottles of whiskey, the kind they hand out on airplanes, all of them full, with unbroken seals. I pick one up and examine it in the afternoon light. Its contents glow golden and a clear air bubble shuttles from the cap to its base. Meredith would say take it so I put it back and close the cabinet. There is no time for that here. But the bottles make perfect sense. My grandfather lived alone in this room with no one to love for twenty-six years. That kind of loneliness takes real strength.

The boys relax against the mango tree trunks shirtless as they wait for my father to return. I should say something. I want to say something, but nothing comes. We live such different lives with such different worries. Who has time to think about sexual orientation when there is no food to eat, no money for school fees, no doctor in sight when you get sick. My father always says we take everything he and my mother have given us too lightly, that people risk drowning in the Caribbean and the Mediterranean for just one-tenth of what we have. He is not wrong. We have studied the Haitians coming to Florida in the nineties in history class. We even had an assembly with a Syrian doctor who told us how he got his family away from ISIS and into Turkey. But I didn't choose my life any more than the boys beneath the mango trees chose theirs, any more than my father chose his.

My father returns just as the sun begins to set and its unraveling colors prompt the frogs and crickets to sing. He pays the boys and instructs Mr. Jacob to give them extra money for waiting so patiently. I watch him from the steps that lead up to the unlit veranda. He thinks they are tough enough to be men, but not me, his own flesh and blood. You should call your mother, he says when he reaches the veranda. We have a big day tomorrow. As he brushes by, his shoes deposit sand onto the newly swept floor.

5

There is hot water by the bathroom door, make sure you bathe today, you hear, my father says when he wakes me the next morning. His phone light throws an unpleasant brightness into my eyes. I can't see his figure behind it but his tone forces me upright immediately. We're going to see Bishop Okereke this morning. Make sure you wear nice clothes.

My mother, OJ and I all agree that the worst part of village life is the bathroom. It has a sloping, moldy cement floor, and a fungus-streaked white tub that emits the most hostile odor, even after a dousing with disinfectant. When I was younger, my mother used to hold her breath while she quickly poured water on me and scrubbed my essential areas. When we got older, OJ and I competed over who could spend the least time in this torture chamber, breath held against the smell, and still come out without soapsuds on our skin or in our hair. OJ always won because he made the point of only washing his face and simply splashing water over the rest of his body. For me, clean meant clean. I never wanted to smell.

A plastic bucket of steaming hot water sits just by the bathroom door made of wood slats held together by a cross beam. The panels are warped from decades of rot. Each year my mother asks my father why he refuses to renovate the house, or at least the bathroom, even after my grandfather has been dead for so long. My father says it's good not to forget some things. I hold my breath and step inside. Sometimes it seems like he just wants to punish someone, anyone, for a long list of grievances that he has never made clear, which you can never ask about because he keeps his emotions so guarded that any question would be interpreted as an assault. I wonder if dragging us to this village and the nearby town where he spent his childhood is a way of sinking us all into his own personal hell so that we can see how this strange combination of poverty and opportunity, these broken and muddy roads, these crumbling houses, these overburdened men and women walking slowly in these streets singing praise songs to keep themselves going, created the strange combination of love and anger and pride and fear that is my father. He always sat in the passenger seat while we drove around the village so he could fully view what he sometimes called a world of wasted opportunity. With OJ or my mother in the car, he pointed out all the things he would make right if only he had the power. With me now, he says nothing. Occasionally he turns to look at me with the same expression that occupies his face when he has to solve a problem at the office. I sink down in my seat and wish that my mother had come.

We arrive at Bishop Okereke's church just as the sun finishes collecting the various colors of the sunrise into one large yellow ball of heat. A handful of people with starved faces stumble from the building, which bears no resemblance to a church. Its long, two-story façade resembles a factory and if not for the phrase, ALL ARE WELCOME, in large gold letters above two massive entrance doors, anyone would mistake it for one. Large stacks of inter-locking tiles for paving the parking lot form a line in front of the building. A yellow Caterpillar earthmover and faded blue grader sit unused at the far edge of the building. I follow my father up the stairs into a large entrance hall lit by dim and flickering fluo-rescent lights. A young woman in a white blouse and black skirt with ill-fitting hair extensions sits at a glass table, atop which rests a large registry filled with scribbles indicating the names and call-ing times of previous visitors. My father signs without saying a word. The woman looks at him, produces two visitor's tags and then gestures to the granite stairs. There is a seat at the top of the stairs just there, she says, Bishop Okereke will find you shortly.

Our footsteps echo as we climb. My father slumps into a low black easy chair set beside a fake-wood coffee table from an office furniture catalog. His face betrays no emotion, but I can tell from the way he lets his head fall onto the seat back that he is tired. When he came home like this, we just left him alone because it was unclear what might make him snap. It could be dirty dishes or the music playing a little too loud, or a dating app on his son's smart-phone that set the world on fire. His blowups did not happen often, but when they did, the consequences were severe and lasting.

The bishop emerges from a security door opposite the couch. He wears a pin-striped suit with an open-collared white dress shirt and recently shined Italian shoes. His stomach bulges against his belt and his cheeks puff out like Dizzy Gillespie's. My father snaps to his feet and takes Bishop Okereke's outstretched hand. The bishop turns to me and with a quick smile says, young man, welcome home. He looks my father up and down. They are the same height, but my father's slender frame makes him appear taller. So my friends, what is troubling you so much that you had to come all the way here to talk to me, Bishop Okereke says. My father glances at the open door. Bishop Okereke nods knowingly and then gestures toward his office. It's just that the air conditioner in my office is broken, he says. My father smiles and stands there until the bishop turns and leads the way.

Bishop Okereke's office is practically empty except for the white lawn table and the two rickety plastic garden chairs he points to. The windows overlooking the muddy parking lot are covered in an elaborate metalwork security screen that forms a cross. A line of red, white and blue checkered Ghana-Must-Go bags line the wall behind the table. One overflows with clerical garments, another reveals the lumpy contours of books. God has blessed us with a new church, Bishop Okereke says, but we have to do the hard work of decorating. My father mutters, Amen. I stare at the bishop's hand and his ring finger swelling around his wedding band. I have never had the guts to say it, but I've always hated the Reverend Olumide, Bishop Okereke style of preacher. They speak and laugh too loud. They project warmth like an industrial heater blasting the closest thing to them with too much intensity instead of radiating like the sun that simply draws you into its warmth. My father grew up Catholic but he always found the church too somber. I liked the Episcopal services at school, calm and thoughtful, preached in quiet voices and punctuated by elegant hymns. I like the idea of God that Jefferson preaches across the pages of our history books—the clockmaker that sets everything in motion but sees no need to intervene. Young man, young man, I hear Bishop Okereke say. My father places his hand on my arm to steady my chair as it rocks. It is the first time he has touched me since the kitchen. I look at my father. He stares directly at the bishop and refuses to return my gaze. Young man, look at me, what your father has told me is very serious, very serious indeed, if it is true, so I'm going to ask you to tell me yourself, have you been engaging in practices of homosexualism. His mouth settles into a prim disapproving line. He shakes his head back and forth slowly as if he wants me to say no, but looks like he is ready to grab my spirit and shake it clean of any faults it may have acquired in its short journey through this world. Answer him Niru, my father says. No, I say directly to Bishop Okereke's face. It's a lie, my father shouts and slams his palm on the scratched white plastic. The whole table bounces and wobbles. It's a lie, he says more calmly a second time. I caught him on his phone. I caught him speaking to other men in some highly disgusting, perverted ways. I saw the filth he keeps on his computer. Of course, he went into my computer. He took everything after he hit me in the kitchen, ripped my laptop from its charging cord, smashed my iPad screen and left the cracked tablet on the kitchen counter. He turns to my father and says, it is good that Reverend Olumide sent you to me. He is right, this demon of homosexuality has become so entrenched in America that you can't really fight it there, some churches are preaching that love of any kind is good while some of them have lost their way and are appointing gays as clergy. You are right to bring him here, this is a place where the faith is strong and hasn't been infiltrated by the devil. I grind my teeth and try to breathe through a growing tightness in my chest. Bishop Okereke says, young man, if what your father says is true, will you confess your sins and rededicate yourself to our Lord and Savior Jesus Christ. If so, it is simple and we know which direction we are going. If not—Bishop Okereke falls silent and folds his arms over his chest—what do you say? I say, I don't know you, so why would I confess anything to you. Niru, my father says. No, it's okay, your son is correct, he doesn't know me, but it is not really me you need to know, it is God. Young man, will you pray with me, with us, Bishop Okereke says, stretching his arms across the table. My father grabs his hand and clutches my arm even though I make no effort to hold him in return. Bishop Okereke's greedy hand flexes its way towards mine. I look at the door. It seems so impenetrable.

People should know when they are conquered, OJ used to say

when he would pin me to the floor and tickle me until I couldn't tell whether I was laughing or crying. There is nothing you can do, give it up, it's easier that way, OJ would say. You can't win, so just let go, he said once when I said I wanted to punch my father in the face. I had only punched one person before, on the soccer field, in eighth grade. It was only later that evening, at home, after I realized that my punishment meant I wouldn't play again that season, that I felt my fingers throbbing and I realized the full impact. Forcing my hands beneath a full flow of first hot water, then burning Listerine, I began to shiver. The idea that I had the potential to wound and destroy inside my body was overwhelming. It unfolded faster than rational thought, underneath a heavy sky and the Cathedral high above. The other boy had an expression of total surprise and anticipation that second before my fist hit his face. That was real power. That is the kind of power that my father understands. What scares me is that he might even appreciate it if I tried to punch his face. He would certainly return the blow without any reservations, even in front of the Bishop. He operates by the doctrine, kill your problems dead so they can't bother you anymore. Sometimes this means violence, sometimes charm, sometimes prayer. Altogether it means Meredith is right and I'm screwed. There is no escaping what my father has brought me here for. There is nowhere to go. Bishop Okereke says, you will come for night vigil in two days' time, then we will see the best way forward.

Mr. Jacob takes us back to the church two nights later. The church lot is half-full when we arrive and guarded by two young men wearing bright yellow reflective vests and armed with large sticks. The ground vibrates from the generators that power the lights in the unfinished church. It stands out against the darkness that covers most of the town and surrounding villages on the hillsides. My father walks solemnly in front of me with his head bowed as if heading to a funeral. I keep my hands in my pockets and remove them every so often to wipe my palms on my slacks. I am nervous. I have been to one all-night prayer vigil before. Reverend Olumide holds them on the last Friday of each month for people to pray their concerns, praise or thanks through the night. My father never goes, but my mother attends at least two each year—one during her birthday month and the other on what would have been my sister's birthday. She always bakes a cake to complement the other potluck dishes and snacks brought by members of the congregation. There are military-style cots lined against the sanctuary walls so that church members can take a break from prayer to rest and recuperate, but the night I went hardly anyone seemed interested in sleep. Reverend Olumide had plugged in an electric kettle at the back and laid out tea, instant coffee and powdered milk so that prayer warriors could keep focus. That night we held each other's trembling hands as we prayed together beneath purposefully dimmed lights. If there was sweat it came from passion; if someone fainted, they were moved by the spirit.

Bishop Okereke's sanctuary is not finished and yet a sizable number of people perch on plastic chairs beneath slow-spinning ceiling fans wobbling on long thin supports hanging from the exposed iron rafters. No cots line the unplastered back walls. No coffeemaker hisses in the background. Instead the generator grumbles and the room swelters with heat it absorbed during the day. A multitude of voices in murmuring prayer rise towards the ceiling where they hang over the soft chords of a highlife guitar and soft hits from the drummer's crash cymbals. The full band is already soaked in their own sweat from singing and praying while dancing to the spirit. Bishop Okereke stands on a makeshift ply-wood riser in his open-collared shirt and no suit jacket. He sees us enter and motions to my father to find a seat in the last empty row of lawn chairs. A few members see his hand signals and break from their prayers to watch us parade down the center aisle. My father keeps his head low until we reach our seats.

Bishop Okereke reads from the Igbo Bible, standing center stage with the large brown book in one hand and his handker-chief in the other. I watch his lips move and feel his words rip-ple through the congregation. I can make out words and some phrases, but he reads quickly and I am lost. My father plays with his hands and picks at his cuticles as he rocks back and forth like a man praying at the Western Wall. I'm not going to give any big sermons tonight, that is for Sunday, Bishop Okereke says. Now is the time for prayer and devotion, for renewal. I invite you to begin your personal journey with God through this night as you are able, those wishing for private spiritual counsel should see one of our prayer warriors. I have never seen my father so agitated. At services he is normally calm; it often looks like he is half-asleep except that he maintains a completely upright posture with his head tilted upwards towards the sound of the word. OJ calls it meditation. But he is not like that here and he has not been calm since the moment we landed in Nigeria. It isn't a positive energy, either. I can feel him scattered, apprehensive, uncertain every time he and I have to share the same space. I'm still me, I want to say to him, your son, but that would hardly help if I am currently everything wrong with the world. How can a man like my father who has done everything right suddenly be saddled with this problem? He has taken our name—the name of a drunken widower and an illiterate older brother—and through sheer force of will made it trusted by people around the world, he has told us. But in the mornings I watch him circle the compound with the slow walk, stopping for a moment each round at his father's resting spot near the orange tree to mutter some words towards the cracked cement slab beneath which he thinks all his dishonor has disappeared. Now I am here and it causes him so much pain. I can see that.

Everyone can see that. And that makes it worse for him. That he has to ask Reverend Olumide for help, that he has to sit in Bishop Okereke's office, that we have to be here now searching for the center of balance on these wobbly plastic chairs arranged in unkempt rows across this hot cement floor is my fault. If only I hadn't said anything to Meredith, if I only hadn't listened to Meredith, I would still be fine—maybe not entirely fine—but before was so much better than this. If I could just make this go away.

My father springs from his seat and charges down the aisle

towards the Bishop as the congregation rises and plastic chairs scrape against the cement. He stands first in line before the Bishop, who without a word, gestures towards the door behind the raised plywood podium. My father follows. I half-stand and then return to my seat. I touch my forehead to the chair in front of me.

I feel a hand on my shoulder. Wake up, wake up, Niru, my father says. He stands above me, his shirt soaked through with his sweat, eyes red and a soiled white towel scrunched in one hand. Listen, it's time, he says. Are we leaving, I say. My father shakes his head. He says, it's time that we . . . He doesn't finish. My mouth dries out and my legs grow weak. I have expected this. I have known it is coming, but I'm not ready. My father says, come on now, we haven't got all night.

There are four people waiting for us in the back room, Bishop Okereke, two women with dull cream-colored fabric draped over their heads, and a small brown man holding a bloated leather-bound Bible with a worn strap positioned standing in a circle at the center of the room. The light bulbs overhead flicker with the fluctuating current from the generator. The room has no windows but a small fan oscillates in the corner. It isn't enough to dispel the heat. Their foreheads shine with sweat. The chamber smells heavily of body odor and cheap perfume. My father pulls the door shut behind us as Bishop Okereke gestures to a spot in the center of the circle, then he squeezes into a corner and bows his head. He does not look at me. Let us pray the Our Father together, Bishop Okereke says, stretching his hands towards his companions. They grip hands and form a trembling circle around me. My father's mouth moves, but I hear no sound. My voice mingles with theirs as our prayers fill the tight space. My shirt grows sticky with my sweat. Please kneel down, young man, Bishop Okereke says. His companions draw closer to me with their hovering palms. My father remains in the corner. Kneel down young man so we can pray over you as God has called us here to do. Do not be afraid, God is in control.

I struggle for breath. My head hurts in the spot where my father bashed my head against the wall. I want to run, but Bishop Okereke's imposing form and his fleshy outstretched palm blocks my path to the door. It feels like they expect people to run. I look around the chamber; there are no whips or shackles, just five other bodies also laboring to breathe in this mix of stale air and body salt. Bishop Okereke's palm pushes my forehead with an otherworldly strength that forces me down. Immediately the man and two women cover my head with their own palms, blocking my view of anything but the cement floor. I feel them vibrating as they warm up with silent murmurs that grow louder as their words give way to unintelligible phrases. I struggle to stand, but someone places a firm hand on my shoulder and holds me down. Their voices grow louder, resonating against the cinder block, in my ears, crashing into my thoughts. I stop trying to stand and instead will my heart to a steady beat. We pray that the evil demonic spirit that seeks to harm this boy's life should leave him and return to the pit of hellfire where it came, Bishop Okereke shouts. Clear out from that place in Jesus's name, another voice says. We ask you to banish the spirit of homosexuality and perversity from this young man, bind it and cast it out in the name of your son, Jesus Christ, Amen. Father almighty destroy each and every unclean thought, untoward desire and abominable notion in the corners of this young mind and heart, refill him with the love of your Word and reverence for your teachings. Fill him Lord Father in the name of Jesus. Father God, reorient this your child to the pure teachings of our Savior Jesus. Unlock in his mind and heart that place where you will reside to protect him from every unclean thing, Bishop Okereke shouts. Protect him Lord, protect him, the prayer warriors echo. Return your child to the spirit of obedience to his parents so that he may hear their direction and heed their advice, the Bishop shouts.

I feel their strength grow the longer they pray. I feel anger expand in my chest, then shame, and then the anger again, now in my stomach. I pray for anything to free me from this room and these hands holding me down, dripping their sweat on me as they try to cleanse me. But also, I want to be clean. I want to be rid of everything that brought me here. I want more than anything to be normal, for my father to say my name with the pride he reserves for OJ's, for him to look at me without disgust, for me to look at him without fear.

Lord as you carry this child back to America, give him the wisdom to see wickedness and the strength to prevail against its many temptations, Bishop Okereke thunders. I feel his words cut into me and I think if only I had seen what Meredith was doing to me. If I only had the strength not to listen to her words. Not that

Meredith is a bad person, but she is a bad influence. She put the app on my phone; she pressured me to go on the date. She was the cause of all this confusion. Bishop Okereke says, take him in your power as his fleshy fingers press my forehead, take him completely in your power Lord and give him control. Give him strength. Give him the power of your everlasting glory. He pushes forward with his hand and throws me back onto the concrete. The light above is blinding and blazes away all the solid figures in the room for a moment while I try to blink my vision clear. As the brightness turns to shapes and the shapes into features, I see shoes and then legs, and then a hand stretching towards mine. My father's face materializes. His cheeks shine with tears. I grasp his hand. He says, come on, get up, let's go home.

6

Washington is different in the spring. Warmer weather draws color from the depths and suddenly there are cherry blossoms. There are other flowers too, daffodils in the brown mulch beds all around the stone buildings, azaleas and roses in the Bishop's Garden. Dandelions spring up in the meadow so the groundskeepers ring the lawn with yellow rope to keep us off while they spray herbicide. My classmates trade chinos for shorts and pasty, hairy legs. They wear loafers with ankle socks or brand-new loosely laced tennis shoes. The girls wear short skirts and short shorts that test the limits of the dress code. Even Ms. McConnell's skirts stop above the knee, so when we walk across the Cathedral to class my classmates talk about fucking her and laugh. I laugh and talk about fucking her too because that is what Reverend Olumide says I should do—except the actual fucking. He says it's okay to be a man and to have the desires that young men have. They are God-given and natural, he says, desire is why babies are made and growing up is God's way of teaching us how to harness desire in the service of his command to go forth and multiply, one man, one woman at a time. He says that I'm scared to grow up so I suppress my desire until it comes out in unhealthy, ungodly ways. Don't be afraid to be a man he says, and to do manly things, but he doesn't say what those are. So I listen to my classmates when they talk about deep throating and donkey punches and I linger on the lawn in front of the Cathedral after class and check out the girls' legs and their asses. Sometimes I feel like something stirs and I think Reverend Olumide is right, but mostly they are just legs and they are just asses, and the words cum slut just don't turn me on. Nothing turns me on and that is just fine for now. I have no need for desire and every need for calm.

The house is calm and has been since we came back from Nigeria. My father doesn't say much beyond questions that require single word answers. Are you hungry? Yes. Have you eaten? No. Did your mother cook? Yes. Will you eat? No. Your homework *nko*? Done. It is as if he considers it his duty to make sure that all my vital functions are under control, but beyond that for now is too much. My mother continues to hover though she tries to be discreet. She is in the kitchen in the mornings, waiting for me with her cup of tea in both hands and eyes that say talk to me, are you okay, why are you punishing me?

You shouldn't eat so fast, she says when I stand by the toaster to wolf down toasted bread smeared with butter. It's not good for your system. She doesn't say anything when I leave my plate on the counter surrounded by a ring of crumbs. Sometimes before I start my car, I hear the sink running. Penance takes different forms, Reverend Olumide says, and I want my mother to feel sorry. You could have prevented this I want to shout at her but instead I let her wash the dishes because I know she doesn't like to.

Those are the good days when I can feel myself fully present and I remember my books for class and I can bullshit through the reading I haven't done, riffing off of classmates by starting my sentences with I feel like or I agree with while Ms. McConnell exclaims, yes. For her my Africanness means I am an authority on all nonwhite things. I watch Meredith roll her eyes at me from across the room. She hasn't been herself recently because college acceptance letters are coming and she is concerned about the rest of her life. We haven't spoken as much because I don't linger after class so I can walk back across the Cathedral lawn with the other boys to discuss manly things. We don't stare into the halogen lights anymore at our spot because Reverend Olumide says I should avoid all triggers.

On good days, I can feel myself growing faster during our speed workouts. Try as they might the other boys can't catch me and I'm a star. I feel the sun warm my skin. I feel my chest burn and expand as if I can inhale the world and exhale my future which I try to catch with each step forward. On good days, Mr. Erickson yells positive things when I tilt out of the curves and unleash down the straightaways. Get 'em son. You got 'em. Ease into it. Relax into it. Everything will work out fine, he says.

But there are also bad days when Ms. McConnell asks me if

everything is okay and I have to bite my lips to keep them from quivering. Class participation is part of your grade, she says to me after class. She gives me extra time to hand in the assignment I didn't do because my father took me to Nigeria. I'm supposed to read *A House for Mr. Biswas* and then I'm supposed to write about home. This should be easy for you, she says and I nod because nodding is easier for her to understand. My classmates joke about Ms. McConnell keeping me after class because she wants some of that big black cock. I laugh because Reverend Olumide says it's okay to behave like a man.

On the bad days, there is no color. I know there are colors. I can see the colors, but the world looks gray. The sounds are muffled by a crackling web of static that sits behind my eyes and buzzes in my ears. Bad days at track make me feel like I'm running through spiderwebs and Coach Erickson tells me to lift my knees and pick my feet up. Do you want it son? It doesn't look like you want it. Show me that you want it. I don't think you want it, son. My chest won't expand and the air I inhale feels like knives cutting me with little swipes from the inside. I feel dizzy as the other boys pass me. This lasts until I get home, where I can fling myself on my bed and wait until everything that is my life—the posters I have tacked to the wall, the paintings of African market scenes my parents have meticulously hung, the over-sweet smell of frying plantain and the one-sided frustration of my mother arguing into the phone in Igbo—stop spinning. Reverend Olumide says I should ask God to be my center so I fall to my knees and beg God. Nothing. My mother hovers. I can see her shadow spread across the landing carpet.

I'm not doing drugs, I tell my mother one morning before I place wheat bread in the toaster. I don't have a gun. Why would you even say such a thing, she says, like she's surprised, but she is not a good liar. It's why she doesn't like working with kids who have cancer. Because someone has been going through my drawers, I say. She doesn't know what to say and instead fills the electric kettle. I take a box of Earl Grey tea from the cupboard over the burner and place it beside her empty mug. No one says anything to me in this house, she says as she pours water over her tea bag. No one tells me things. Reverend Olumide says men are about doing, not talking. We do, it's what we do, he says. Mommy, I'm not doing drugs, I repeat. I'm going to be late for school.

Everyone at school is unsettled. Those of us who got into college early have known our fates for months now, but the rest who valued choice over certainty or didn't fare so well in the early admissions bounce around with nervous excitement. There are rumors that rejection letters come first, even if only by a millisecond. There are stories of computer glitches that sent acceptance letters to a whole swath of unworthies and lawsuits from parents that allege irreparable psychological harm. I like the term unworthies as it gets tossed about. It makes me feel like I am somebody. It makes this one day in April feel almost religious, if only once in your life.

Ms. McConnell knows there will be no learning today. She

says her classroom is open to those interested in free reading and conversation. She says she is here for support. There is a large bowl of silver Hershey's Nuggets on her desk. My classmates help themselves before exiting to walk and talk their anticipation off in front of the Cathedral. Ms. McConnell sighs because wealth does not equate to good manners. All the desks are empty but Meredith's seems more so than the others because her sloppy posture makes her body fill more space than it should, because she has a feeling about almost everything we read and discuss, and because she is loud about those feelings. Without her, life is quiet. With her it is often unbearably loud. Niru, you're welcome to stay if you want, Ms. McConnell says to me without looking up from her desk. Without students in her classroom she is much smaller and more feminine. I stare at her legs visible beneath her desk and at the way her blond hair falls about her face as she reads the *New Yorker*. Porn makes it look so easy, so casual, so routine. Older women are supposed to crave fresh young meat, to lick their pen tops absentmindedly while thinking about us, to squeeze their legs together in a good faith effort to keep from corrupting the younger generations. And I am supposed to stumble forward both confused and uncontrolled, pulled by my relentless desire like light towards a black hole. Except I am unmoved. I imagine Ms. McConnell naked, perched at the edge of her desk, legs crossed waiting for me to cross the room and give her what she needs. That's how they always say it, that they will take what they want, get what they need, that hardcore sex is good punishment for bad behavior. I wonder if it would set the record straight for me.

It's nice outside, Ms. McConnell says, you should enjoy the day. Her stare makes me feel like she can read my thoughts and I am suddenly embarrassed. Or maybe she simply wants a moment to do what teachers do when they are alone, pick her nose, scratch that itch that couldn't be scratched discreetly while standing in front of fourteen irreverent, entitled souls. Either way I quickly gather my belongings and leave. She offers me chocolate on the way out but I say no thank you.

The Cathedral grounds are quiet between the waves of tourists. I wander aimlessly along the paths between the knolled lawn and large oak trees, taking care to avoid stepping on the cracks between large slabs of white concrete. I sit on a bench given in memory of some loving but now dead couple. I watch squirrels chase each other around mulch beds and in spirals up tree trunks. The grounds crew has sprayed the brown edges of the lawn with green fertilizer where they meet the path. From high above it must look like unparalleled perfection, but from a few feet away it's clear that you can't paint over your blemishes. The fertilizer is too green for the actual grass.

Meredith is not at the buttress. I slide down against the limestone, pull the cheap Nokia phone my mother gave me from my pocket and dial her number. The architecture amplifies each beep from my phone and each ring from hers. When she doesn't answer, I figure she wants to be alone with her thoughts. It's a cruel trick of fate to have admissions letters sent on the day of our first track meet. It makes you feel like God sometimes just wants to fuck with people, or like admissions officers and track coaches want to test your faith in God. Meredith has held faith for the last five months that Harvard will have faith in her— even after the initial early deferral. They have to. She is smart and her parents are important. I wait for a few moments to see if she'll call me back. When she doesn't, I brush off my pants and head to the locker room. Reverend Olumide says that I should spend more time around people. He says activity helps to keep untoward thoughts at bay.

The locker room is already full when I arrive and someone's phone blasts trap music through speakers stolen from the computer lab. The sound bounces off the cream-colored cinder blocks and vibrates against metal locker doors. There are so many bodies in this tight space that I can feel the temperature rise as soon as I step inside, or maybe it's the steam from the showers, or maybe it's just me. I have been in locker rooms before and I have been in this locker room before with these same people, but of course now it's different, just as everything has been different since the blizzard. You cannot unsee what has been seen once the veil is lifted, Reverend Olumide says in church. We cannot return to the garden of Eden. When I meet with him he says I need to confront my fears, that the devil torments us with that which scares us most. So, I cross the line between the blue hallway tiles and the white locker-room floor and navigate my way through a series of fist bumps and handshakes to locker number thirty-two. It's the top half of a standing pair usually reserved for the underclassmen fast enough, lucky enough or brave enough to snatch a spot of seniority on the team. I should have a full locker but my indecision at the beginning of the season as to whether I would brave the bodies has cost me dearly. The locker is in the corner by the grated frosted window and there are so many bodies to navigate if I want to get out. The music is loud in this space and distorted as it ricochets against the corner walls—the team playlist, "Jumpman" for the high jumpers, followed by "I'm on a New Level" because Adam, our captain, is a high jumper. Four skinny, pasty sophomores practice dabbing shirtless in the showers. There is an economy sized tub of protein powder perched precariously on one of the benches before them. I have always been jealous of people who are comfortable being naked. I undo my tie and slip off my shirt.

Hey Harvard, Adam shouts. He has called me that ever since early admissions were announced in December. I can't see with my shirt halfway over my head but I can tell he is somewhere behind me. Where's your girlfriend going to college, he says. I swallow hard and feel the fact that I haven't eaten breakfast or lunch deep in my stomach. For the first time today I'm dizzy. Caught in the whiteness of my undershirt, I feel like I'm about to fall. I touch my hand to the wall for support. It slips against the condensation from the showers. Someone shouts that he has to take a shit. The mixtape blasts "Fuck Up Some Commas" because the white boys find the thought of black people rapping about grammar funny. I slip my shirt over my head and spin around. Adam wears only spandex. He is tall and muscular but his face is still very young. He knows he has nice abs and he has worked to build his calves and thighs. He smiles mischievously. You know, Meredith, he says. I stare at him without blinking. My mouth won't work. I need to take a shit. The one who you're too afraid to fuck, he says. He's not afraid, he just likes it in the butt, Rowan says. The room is silent because the mixtape stops and the only words to echo belong to the person who has made my existence uncomfortable since the first day we met. I can't look at him because he feeds off discomfort. He is the shark that senses blood in the water, the growling dog that knows you've stopped dead in your tracks. I want to punch him, but I have seen these fights play out multiple times and have no desire to end up grappling in the showers while the rest of the team eggs us on as they record everything with their phones. There was a scandal last year that involved a lacrosse team brawl posted on World Star Hip Hop. The Headmaster was livid. Students were suspended. He called an assembly to remind us that we just don't do that here. I want to look at Rowan to confirm he still has his small hate-filled blue eyes and his permanent I'm-out-of-fucks-to-give smirk. He's going to be an alcoholic, I tell myself. He's going to divorce his third wife and need a liver transplant. He will go bald prematurely and get an STD from a meth-addicted prostitute. The toilet flushes. I say, shut the fuck up. OJ says you can only feel your skin at your best and worst moments so right now I can feel all of my skin, on my fingers, on my face, full of itch and fire. Rowan barks a vicious laugh that always makes Ms. McConnell clench her fists and breathe deeply. He says, that's not what Meredith would say. My chest collapses. I can only see white.

Meredith stands in the corner with a beer in her hand but she's not smiling. Her nails are painted purple and gold like her teammates but she didn't run today. She didn't even show up. She hasn't returned my calls and she won't look at me. I can't stop staring at her. She holds her beer like a professional, like a woman in a commercial with long beautifully delicate but strong hands. Her top has spaghetti straps and plunges down the back so she can't wear a bra. With eyeliner, mascara and lip gloss highlighting her features, she looks a little older, a little more sophisticated and more noticeable. Rowan has noticed her. He keeps watching her with his tiny eyes. He holds a cup full of punch, then he holds two cups full of punch. Then he holds a cup of punch and a beer. He wears a Princeton hat because that's where he will go next year, but it is old and tattered because he has always worn a Princeton hat because he has always known he is going there. That is why he never has any fucks to give—because his family can afford not to give them. He holds two cups of punch again and stands at the edge of a granite kitchen countertop scattered with plastic cups, beer cans and plastic bags full of melting ice, tapping his fingers against their red ridges so some of the liquid spills onto his small hands. He watches Meredith toss her long brown hair over her shoulder so that we can see the single diamond stud suspended just beneath her collarbones on a thin gold chain. She rolls it between her fingers and it makes her look delicate and pretty. Rowan thinks she does it to look pretty because he thinks all women do all things to look either pretty or fuckable. He has always thought Meredith pretty. Now he thinks her fuckable. I know she touches her necklace when she's agitated or nervous because it reminds her of her grandmother and her grandmother made her feel safe. Rowan moves toward her with two beers. I choose to go outside.

Washington, D.C. is so confusing in the spring. The days grow increasingly hot and humid, but the nights hold on to winter for as long as possible. On some days the grass is still frosted over in the mornings, stiff and crunchy, even if it wilts before the first class starts. If you are not careful you get caught in the weather's nostalgia and at night, a windbreaker or sweater isn't enough. Adam wears a T-shirt as he stands with two girls and another guy who all go to another school. Adam drapes his arm around one of the girls, who has wrapped her hands in her thin sweater sleeves and her arms around his body. Still she shivers. The garden table before them is littered with red cups and a bottle of Absolut. The other girl pours a little in each cup. Then she looks at me. You want some, she asks. Adam looks up and cheers. He says, after your race today, you should celebrate, I've never seen anyone come from behind like that, you totally should have come in first. I would have come in first if my legs hadn't faltered in the last hundred meters, and if I had eaten breakfast or lunch. I started off weak, distracted by my body, my hamstrings hurt, my knees hurt, and my chest felt tight from the locker room. Coach Erickson thought I should have won. He pulled me aside while I was trying to find my breath and said, if you're going to run then really run, you're not going to get anywhere if you keep holding back. Thanks man, I mumble to Adam. I turn around to go back inside. Oh come on, you're not going to drink with us Harvard, Adam says. Drink, drink, drink, he chants and the others join in. The girl in the sweater mixes vodka and Coke in a red cup. It's my vodka, she says and smiles. Drink up.

You're not like these white children, my mother says, so don't go and follow their foolishness. But according to my father I am already foolish, irredeemably foolish. I look at these kids laughing with each other, standing without jackets like even the cold can't touch them and I don't understand why there are people for whom rules and norms are fully optional, for whom foolishness is celebrated. There are kids smoking weed in the basement of someone's parents' house and there are kids fucking in the bathroom. There are kids who have brought little vials of cocaine that I can't even imagine where they came from. And there is me, black, sober and scared to death by locker room banter from an epic asshole. There is also me, the senior in the spring on a Friday. I will have the rest of my life to be constricted and I will have the rest of my life to make amends.

Reverend Olumide says there is no growth without risk. He says that young men should do the things that young men do.

I say, okay and take the red cup from her red painted fingernails. Adam and his friends cheer. The alcohol swims underneath the Coke and it doesn't burn and it doesn't taste. It is the first thing that is not water to hit my stomach. There you go, Harvard, Adam shouts. He rubs my back while the sweater girl with red nails wraps her arms around him tighter. He kisses her mouth and she receives him eagerly. He hands me another cup. Drink, drink, drink, drink, swallow it down Harvard, swallow it down, and he is laughing, and they are high-fiving with me, fist-bumping with me, hugging me until I am no longer myself, but a part of something more. Swallow it down, you've got to swallow it down, they say until the cups are empty and my fingers no longer feel cold when they hold Adam's shoulder because the world is tilting and foggy and twisting suggestions and shapes of things like the silhouette that shouts, pizza, from the light filled doorway, holding boxes up high. Let's eat, Adam says. Snooze you lose, sweater girl says and the other girl grabs my hand with her soft hands and leads me to the light. You don't want to lose. No I don't, I don't want to lose but I am lost already amongst the so many people crowding everywhere, sitting on every surface without red cups and light bottles and dark bottles and boxes and cans that I don't touch because I hate the smell of beer as my feet stick and unstick to the floors. I have lost her hand in all the madness, and in the madness, I have found more fist bumps and handshakes and high fives until someone shouts, wassup my nigga, because drunk white kids think imitating black people is hilarious. The walls pulse and now a circle clears beneath a high-hanging sparkling chandelier so the track team can try to dance "I'm On a New Level," like black people because the way black people move, to them, is funny. You're on a new level, right, Adam says with his palms to my temples and his forehead to my forehead blowing hot breath that smells of beer and his girl's glitter-gloss kisses. I am on a new level, a landing one flight up when suddenly there is Meredith's diamond flashing like an accusatory all-seeing eye. You're here, I say, she nods with tight lips and no smile and a red cup in her hand. But you weren't there, at the track meet, why not at the track meet? Because I needed self-care, I didn't get in. You didn't get in to? To Harvard. Omygodimsosorry Meredith. Niru, what the fuck, she says and leaves her lips parted with her disbelief. Where have you been? I've been here. Not as my friend you haven't. You avoid me after class. I text. You don't text back. I call. You don't call back. I called you today, I say. The boys have gotten louder. They are on a new level and we can hardly hear ourselves above the drink, drink, drink, and all the cheers. She pulls me upstairs and I stumble so she stumbles. The carpet is soft against the hand that catches me. We're on a new level and it's quieter so I feel like déjà vu. What's wrong with you Niru? Did I do something else? I said I was sorry, she says as she rolls her diamond and speaks in a small voice that I almost can't hear. I can see her face clearly now and how it's twisted and pained beneath her eye shadow and lip gloss. Every time I tell you something, something goes wrong. What did I do now? You told Rowan. Huh, she says. Her mouth is an *O*, like she is confused, but there is no sound. She says, I don't get it. You told Rowan about me, I know you did. I didn't say shit to Rowan, why would you say that? My stomach turns and turns. Her red cup quivers in her hands between her gold and purple painted fingernails and her face is red. Then why did he say so to me in the locker room, before the meet you skipped because you care for yourself. I can't believe you think I would tell Rowan. Then how would he know? I don't know. Stop lying. Fuck you Niru, just fuck you, she says and she is crying a little as she twists her diamond to her lips as she backs away and turns around so I see her bare shoulder blades beneath the thin spaghetti straps. Her freckled skin makes me angry, so angry and my stomach turns as the white boys downstairs fuck up some commas, laughing at black boys like me but with bad grammar. Meredith, I shout and burp and feel a wave of hot alcohol breath and bile rise and pull and subside just like when I was four and all I wanted, all I ever wanted was just to have some Coke but she is starting down the steps until she is not because my hand circles her arm and her bare skin feels strangely warm even if her muscles are hard and frozen. You can't just fuck everything up, literally everything and just walk away.

She is scared. Her eyes flash across my face, looking for something in my face to help her decide: threat or not, fight or flee? Inhale, breathe, you, yes me, I, not her, am the victim here. I clutch my hand to my belly and squeeze her arm for support because all these things are too much to stomach all alone, especially in the twisting and tilting and the rising noise coming from below. Let me go, she says. She says, let me go, I didn't make you gay. This world is so unfair, so very unfair my knotted stomach says to my brain and to my hands which clench around her flexed muscles, but now with anger and as her eyes search my face again, now with rage. Well maybe Harvard didn't take you cause you're a lying ass-face. There is no more color in her face and then I cannot see her face because my eyes burn, but I hear her red cup crack and I hear Rowan cheer, drink, drink, drink, even if I cannot see through the pain or hear through all the voices, swallow it down, swallow it down, swallow it down, this rage, swallow me down from this embarrassment, this misery, from all these surrounding faces that can look but can't see what has happened, what she has done. Fight or flee. Now that I can see, I can see only one way out away from here, from these white boys and white girls and their wassup my nigga madness, past Adam and his red-nailed glitter-gloss-lipped appendage and Rowan's curious, hateful, beady eyes through all the bodies, giving pounds, throwing up high fives until the doors open to let me away with speed so I can run, yes really run, away into the darkness before me, into this night where the air stings my face. I need to stop and really breathe. No such luck. My legs carry me through this world of swirls, wobbling this way that way lurching left correcting right, tripping over my own imaginary untied shoelaces like some oversized toddler mid-tantrum. I mumble to myself through my own stiffness and tears, about myself, about the world as my whole body burns.

Then there are so many lights and so many bodies, some arm in arm, on the brick sidewalks in front of the shops and banks and more shops and restaurants on M Street where the college students in skinny jeans that make their butts look big and their ankles small above their sneakers and boots, and the medical students, and law students, and graduate students and yuppies who wear dress shoes as casually as they can, all walk. It all makes my head hurt and my head spin and my stomach churn like I am nervous. But I am not nervous. Not here. Not anymore. Not now. All that has been said has been said. What more can be spoken? I am tired and nauseous. I stop to rest against a lamppost while the people on foot and in cars and buses pass me by. My shoelaces have come undone and my intestines are unraveling. The sidewalks undulate with each step and cars rumble around me.

I can feel it before I smell it, and then smell it before I taste it, the cold shiver and prickling, then the acid hot burn of the vodka and the Coke that rises to force me to my knees and then the purge, and the purge, and the purge. Are you okay? Of course you're not okay. Nah, nah, stay down, stay down, says a voice that comes at me from every direction and I want to stay down but can someone tell me which way is down? There are so many shoes, Jordans, boots, loafers, cream-colored high heels and then Jordans closer, attached to ankles wrapped tight in skinny jeans. Should we call an ambulance, I think he needs an ambulance. No I want to shout, no ambulances, they are for the sick and the dead, and I am still living, not dead even though I will be if my parents have to leave whatever function they attend to find me lolling about a cot in an emergency room in clothes stiff with my own dried vomit. I stand up. I am fine, I'm okay. But I'm not okay. You're a hot mess, say the Jordans. My vomit pools in a dip of the sidewalk. The Jordans step back and I wipe my hands against my pants until they are no longer sticky. No hospital. No, please, no, I'm okay. He's gonna be all right, no ambulance? Nah

I don't think—Gosh these kids think they can just come to this neighborhood and do whatever, we should really call the police. Nah, no need. Do you know him then? The voice is angry for no reason, like everything is too small for everybody all at once and only the strong survive. I'm calling the police, let them take care of him. It's okay, I got him. Can you stand? I can stand—in your arms yes, yours, if you hold me I think, but my mouth doesn't move because his face is so concerned and kind with his light brown almost green eyes and his voice so soft and familiar. Can you walk? I can walk—if you hold me, if you hold my hand in your hand and lead me. I work in this store right here, we've got a bathroom in the back, I'm a help you back there and you can clean yourself up. Can you walk? I can walk, I think.

The bathroom is small with air full of freshener and disinfectant, fancy soap in a fancy bottle, something organic, something environmental perched on the rim of a sturdy industrial sink. I grab the sink. I hold on to the sink as more of my life forces itself out of me. I want to rinse my mouth, but the top looks rusted and the rush of water looks full of rust and heavy metals. My face burns, and my lips burn. I touch two fingers to the flow and then to my lips. The rich man begged God from hell to let Lazarus slake his thirst with just two drops but God said certain torments are eternal. I dab at my forehead with my wet palms. I wet paper towels and scrub the vomit on my clothes. Stupid. You are stupid, my father would say because no son of his could do the things I've done, the things I do. I can't see straight enough to see one version of myself in the scratched mirror before me. And

I can't think straight enough to remember where I put my keys, this pocket or that pocket, this pocket, yes. And my car? I slam my palms against the wall. Again. The skin turns pink. You are not like these white children, my mother says except on my palms that turn pink like their skin turns pink, but only when hurt, or scared or stressed. There are taps on the door, Are you okay in there? Imokayjustaminute, someone says and that someone is me. Take your time, no problem, just wanted to make sure you're still alive in there, that you hadn't collapsed cause that would be bad. I'm okay, I'm fine. I put a change of clothes on the floor out here if you need them. Thankyousomuch. My shoes stink of vomit even in all the air freshener and antiseptic and soap. I take them off and hold the tops beneath the gushing faucet. Outside the door there are folded gray sweats. Then I am naked. Then I wear the sweats and feel their fuzz against my skin, against my chest and my back and my inner thighs. You have to, have to, get this shit, you have to get under control, I hear myself tell myself as I take my phone and wallet from my vomit-streaked pants and slip them into the pockets of the sweat pants. Yes, yes, myself agrees. The self in the mirror, his red eyes swim in liquid and they bulge from his face. What a horribly ugly face. What a stupid simple face, with its open mouth and big lazy lips shining with drool. Close your mouth, don't be a gollywog, my father used to say, don't be a big-lipped gollywog, but I didn't know what that was. It sounded sweet and friendly, but now I see myself I know what that means and I can't look any longer. Idiot. Abomination. Not myself. Not my father's son. Nothing. Nobody to no one. Nonce.

You good, he asks me with lips so full and eyes drowned by concern. I touch my chest. I can't pay, I can't pay for these—no money, I say. Don't worry, seriously. I shuffle to the front of the store very unsteady. It all takes so much effort, each step a separate command and each action a deliberate thought. Now move, Niru. Now stop. Now breathe. There is no vomit on the sidewalk. Someone has washed me away.

Can you get home, he asks. His skin is soft brown and his hair wavy jet-black. My heart stops. Home? Where is home? I feel sick again. The world spins again. It's all right, it's okay. Do you have a license? Yessir, yes sir, in my pocket. Do you have a phone? Yes, yessir in my other pocket. Damn I ain't seen one of these in years, what's this? It's a phone. No this is a call-making device. He is funny but if I laugh my stomach swims and if my stomach swims I will vomit again. I'll get you an Uber. You don't have to. Oh I do, you're a hot mess. I'm so sorry. No problem, we've all been there. But have we?

Then there is an Uber with black doors and gray pleather seats. The satellite radio speaks in Amharic to the driver, who looks at me through his rearview mirror. He asks, what's the best way to go? I say I don't know as I slump down in the back seat, crack the window and feel the cold air wash over me.

The house is dark when we pull up and I remember the spare key under the mat at the basement door. My sneakers squish as I cross the lawn. I sit down to remove them because I don't want to soil my mother's carpets. I touch my forehead to the cool glass door panes and stare into the darkness to see what waits for me.

7

I can't remember his face, but I think about him before I sleep. Sometimes it's his eyes sometimes his hands, sometimes his Jordans, sometimes his voice. I know him only in fragments and I can't erase those fragments. They torment me. I say nothing to Reverend Olumide, who tells me that he is thrilled with the progress we are making. He says the struggle to live with the Lord is lifelong and constant. He tells me to pray always for deliverance. You don't have to be alone in this, he says. The weather is warmer so he wears short sleeves and shirts unbuttoned at the collar. He tells me to stay vigilant, that temptation will still come. He writes down Bible verses for me to read, on white index cards in dark blue ink with letters almost as perfect as a computer's. I take the cards—Genesis 4:7, Luke 5:32, First Corinthians 6:18—and put them in my pocket without looking at them. I have a stack on a shelf in my closet. They remind me of all the things I should do.

I don't do them. Instead, on days when practice ends early,

I take the long way home, detouring through Georgetown and lodging myself in the slow-rolling traffic on M Street so that I pass the store where he works. From my car, I see the faceless mannequins in runners' spandex leggings and neon sports bras leaving exposed milky white mannequin midriffs. I see running shoes stacked high to the ceiling and the trickle of white-haired men and old but fit women who can afford the thirty percent location markup on a pair of shoes. The workers wear black shirts. I see them in fragments through the crowded display case, an arm here, the back of a brown head, a ponytail. I want the whole. I'm drawn to the whole, but I drive on overwhelmed by my embarrassment. My sneakers curve upwards like banana boats because I ran them through the wash.

My father wanted to buy a new battery for my car after I told my parents that I took an Uber home when the engine wouldn't start. He insisted on coming with me to retrieve it from school and frowned with confusion when the car started immediately after I turned on the ignition. Maybe it's the spark plug, he said. I said, we should get home and look at it there. I had a headache and my stomach still felt uneasy. My father followed close behind me in his Range Rover. My palms were sweaty against the steering wheel.

Each time I pass, I tell myself that tomorrow I will stop, but when tomorrow comes I don't stop because I'm scared. The devil always comes in fragments until you experience eternity in its consuming entirety, Reverend Olumide says. I say the next day I will stop because random acts of kindness should not go unrecognized, but the next day comes and I can't piece together what I would say to those eyes and I drive on, past the Key Bridge and up MacArthur Boulevard where I roll down my windows and inhale the spring smells of wet earth and new leaves, and sometimes scream into the passing wind so that my voice is hoarse and my throat sore when I get home. Since when did you start drinking so much tea, my mother asks me, every day tea, tea tea, as if tea is going out of fashion, she says. But I know she is secretly proud because she likes that I am adopting one of her British habits.

Meredith would know what to do but we don't speak anymore so I can't ask her for help. Instead we sit across from each other in Global Literatures trying desperately not to look like we're not looking at each other. She is different now. Her skirts and shorts are shorter now and she wears more makeup. Rowan tries not to look like he's looking at her and Adam teases me after class. Dude you should totally hit that, you saw her cross and uncross her legs, it's like *Basic Instinct*, he says, you know the movie with Sharon Stone. He likes movies so I nod and smile as we walk and he bounces. Rowan pulls fraying threads from the bill of his Princeton hat, but he says nothing. I want to hate him but it's a waste of time. He wouldn't give a fuck anyway.

I text Meredith with my Nokia, cycling through letters and numbers with excruciating slowness and I hope she knows this means I'm serious. She doesn't respond. I call Meredith after class but she ignores me. During my free period I walk up Wisconsin

Avenue to the drugstore to look for blank greeting cards and Dum Dums. An older white woman with thinned gray curls and wrinkles badly covered by too much makeup rings me up. She smiles at me when she scans my items and while the register beeps, she says, I know it's spring when you boys start coming here with your blazers looking for candy. In my day, the boys gave us flowers. I smile and swipe my card quickly. I hope she's worth it, she says with a wink. My father thinks all white people in service jobs are stupid, bitter and mean, but she seems perfectly normal, maybe a little sad.

I draw stick figures in comic book squares on every available surface of the greeting card. They talk about when we were younger and we killed time doing silly things like staring directly into the halogen bulbs at the base of the Cathedral and then stumbling about blinded by faith, Meredith said. I drew all the waiting after orchestra for our parents to come while Lonnie the Bahamian security guard asked us, ya parents coming soon? I leave it on her sports bag during practice. Is it too late to say I'm sorry, I write. Meet me after practice in the meadow, I text, but Meredith doesn't come to the meadow, not after fifteen minutes, not after the street is empty and all the boys have gotten into their cars and gone home, leaving me standing in the perfect grass, alone.

There are still colored streaks in the sky when I leave. The sunset shimmers in the windows of the Russian embassy and the storefronts lining Wisconsin Avenue so that the whole city looks like stained glass. OJ loved evenings like this when the world seemed perfect and he would drive us home playing underground hip-hop, rapping along softly while tapping his thumbs against the wheel. But he hasn't been here for some time and normally he is too busy to talk on the phone. I know that my parents have told him nothing of the last few months, my mother out of concern for me, my father for shame, both because OJ needs to focus if he wants to become an orthopedic surgeon, and my issues are an unwelcome distraction. I dial his number and listen. Somewhere in New York, "Call Tyrone" plays and my brother either ignores it or is busy. His half-Nigerian girlfriend gifted him the ringtone. She is also a medical student so my mother is willing to overlook her whiteness. She called my mother to wish her a Merry Christmas. She texted me too. They go to church on the Sunday mornings they aren't in the hospital. I cut the phone before it goes to voice mail. No, he wouldn't understand.

There is a part of me that wishes Sportzone would burn down, leaving nothing but a sticky mess of rubber soles and melted mannequins with blistered and charred skin, but the only one capable of incinerating problems is God and almost everyone who matters in my life tells me that God is not on my side. I know I should go home right away, because that's what is expected of me, that's what OJ would do, what good sons do. There are normal things that normal people do at normal times, I heard my father tell OJ once when he called a girl his girlfriend. OJ was thirteen, so he sat in the front seat of my father's car. I was seven so I sat in the back like I wasn't even there. I played with the straps on my backpack as we sped home. OJ squirmed like he wanted nothing more than to leave right then, forget the cars and moving vehicles driving by. His fingers slid against the silver door latch, then under it as his hand tensed to pull it back, but he let it go. I don't fight battles I can't win OJ tells me when I complain about our parents. It makes life less difficult.

I park beneath a dogwood tree on Thirty-Second Street. Its smell immediately fills the car. Someone on the girls' track team called them "cum trees"—she said their blossoms smell like semen. I wonder how many people put our noses to that dip between our index fingers and thumbs that night. The name stuck and now dogwoods make me think of sex. Thinking about sex is normal, Reverend Olumide says, but certain kinds of sex are not. Pray for strength. Pray for deliverance. Petals fall from the tree when I shut the door. A light breeze shakes more loose. The car will be covered with them by the time I get back, but there are no other parking spots. I'm out of options.

I hesitate at the glass door to Sportzone while the mannequins watch me with their hands on their hips and brand-new running shoes on their feet. Inside bright fluorescent light floods over sportswear neatly folded on industrial metal tables. Different shoe styles climb the wall on small wooden shelves arranged by brand, purpose and pattern: darks at the bottom, light colors at the top. Their distorted reflections shimmer in the high-gloss concrete floor.

A lone salesgirl with a microphone earpiece and a soccer player's ponytail leans on a compact stand with an iPad for checkout. She looks at me, briefly less bored but also trained well enough to know that my purchasing power is not worth adjusting her perkiness level. How can I help you, she says. I scan the store but there is no one else inside. I can't remember much from my first time inside except for the colors and the cold air forced down with a hiss from the exposed vents above. I just, I wanted to take a look at some running shoes, I say. Knock yourself out, she says. I do need new shoes. My current pair are less malleable after their session in the washer-dryer, but I have been afraid to ask my parents for money. I don't want to ask them for anything. I lift a neon-blue trainer with red reflective stripes from its platform and turn it over—one hundred and eighty dollars. Everything in the store is thirty percent off, a voice says. I freeze like I have just stepped on a glass shard. He is shorter than me and he has a fresh shape-up, well-oiled so the sharp line of brushed-forward hair contrasts sharply with his brown skin. I swallow at his confused smile. Focus. But that smile. But those eyes. Focus. He has seen me, really seen me and still his gaze is insistent. Do I smell, yes I smell, but he has already smelled the worst of me. This is torture. What beauty, a solid frame of sculpted arms and broad chest made all the more broad by his fitted black golf shirt, collar popped. Focus. On what—straight ahead to his face? But those lips. Say a prayer to slow this fast-beating heart? But his strong, delicate hands. To wet this dry mouth? But the soft slope of his nose. For deliverance? You're back, he says now settled fully into his smile and this secret familiarity. Feeling better?

He has such a wicked smile, with perfect teeth and just the right amount of arrogance. I feel the shoe slip from my sweaty hands as my legs grow weak. Well, you came to the right place for shoes, he says. How much running are you planning on doing? Here, have a seat and maybe I can help you find something.

Then shoeboxes surround us as he talks to me about running. He says his name is Damien and that he studies dance at Howard University but he wants to move to New York to dance with Alvin Ailey. I don't know what that is but I nod all the same. He watches me as I walk around the store weaving through the metal tables with a different style of shoe on each foot. He asks me how they feel but I can't feel anything at the moment. Like I'm floating, I say. Which one, he asks. I point to the neon-blue shoe with red stripes even though the instep feels narrow. Good, he says, trust your judgment. He squats down in front of me to probe for space between my toe and the front of the shoe. You don't want it to be too snug so your feet can expand the more you run. If you're sure, I can get them from the back, he says as he scans the shoe with his phone. You can pay Lisa up front.

The blond-haired girl looks at me with greater interest when I approach, my debit card already in hand. I hope you found what you were looking for, she says, with a wide smile. I nod as she swipes my card and swivels her iPad so I can sign. My mother will ask me about the price, then she will ask me if I think money falls from the sky like manna. When I look at Lisa, I can breathe freely again until Damien returns with the box and a smile. Thank you, I say as I back away from him towards the door. Out on the street the traffic has thinned, but an older man in a Mercedes convertible plays Bob Dylan really loud, buses lumber past and a young woman in bright yellow shorts and pale legs jogs by. She is so skinny that her knees buckle outwards as she moves. No, the world has not changed.

Someone taps my shoulder. Damien stands in front of me holding a small white square of paper that flutters with the evening breeze. You forgot your receipt, he says, extending his hand just as a car approaches from behind, setting his body aglow. My fingers touch his fingers as I take the paper. I see that he feels me. Thank you, I say again, and also for the other night. Don't mention it, he says. Have a good night. Then he is gone.

I hold the paper as I walk back to my car. No, the world has not changed, but my arms quiver. I unfold it before I unlock the door. His number floats across the white strip and I realize the smell of dogwoods doesn't bother me.

8

My new life begins with coffee. That is what Damien and I decided when I finally dialed the number on the receipt. I sat beneath the flying buttress holding my phone. It took three tries entering the ten digits on my Nokia with trembling hands before the voice in my head saying stop was drowned out by the parade of young mothers and nannies in SUVs picking up their squeaking little ones from school. Carpe diem bitches, Adam liked to say ever since we read *Romeo and Juliet*. I pressed send.

He sounded like he had just woken up and I imagined him laid out on white sheets in a white room with sunlight streaming in through large windows, white curtains billowing in the breeze. Then he sneezed. It's me Niru. Oh right, Niru. What's up. I just thought I'd call to—Thanks for calling. I thought maybe I got it really wrong. I held my breath and said nothing as an irate mother honked at another mother to please move. Yeah, I just wanted to say thank you for the shoes, they're perfect. That's cool. I said, cool, watching a lone kid with an oversized backpack shuffle the sidewalk a few paces ahead of his anxious father. Stay with me, Peter, the father yelled. Okay, well I guess, I'll talk to you later, he said. Can I see you, I said without warning, without thinking, surprising myself. He said, yeah sure, tomorrow, like around now? He asked, have you been to Tryst, you'll like Tryst.

Now I stand across Eighteenth Street from my future staring up at large brown letters boldly painted on a cream-colored pediment. The sun shines so customers spill through sliding doors to sidewalk tables set beneath large red umbrellas. They pretend to work at laptops but pay more attention to people walking up and down the sidewalk. Carpe diem, I say and step into the street.

Inside there are people everywhere, clustered together at communal tables, facing each other on mismatched chairs and sunk comfortably into sagging couches removed from living rooms and basements. The college students study each other and the street over their laptop screens and textbooks. They raise their phones to text every other minute. Other customer tribes claim the cafe's different quarters. There are Ethiopians at the round tables and hard benches near the bathrooms and young mothers in the paired easy chairs with space enough between them to fit a stroller. The couches are full of young single people hoping to brush an attractive stranger accidentally on purpose while reaching down to the floor sockets to plug in their laptops or phones. And there is Damien at the far end of the coffee bar that runs the length of the café. He sits on his hands hunched over a book laid flat on the counter, between a half-eaten chocolate chip cookie and a glass of milk. He sees me in the mirror above the bar and smiles. He wears jeans with holes at the knees. His white T-shirt glows with sunlight reflected from the mirror across the bar and he wears brand-new red running shoes. I catch my reflection in the mirror, rumpled khakis, wrinkled blue dress shirt, blazer. I could have tried harder. You're here, Damien says. His voice rises and falls with a casual elegance that it doesn't have at Sportzone. He closes his book and breaks off a piece of cookie. His actions are deliberate, nothing wasted in the flow of hand to cookie to mouth to glass of milk to mouth to dabbing away his milk mustache with a folded brown paper napkin. He pats the empty stool beside him and rests his chin on his fist while he watches me. I hesitate. You're new at this, Damien says, don't worry, it gets better. Does it, I ask. It did for me, once I left home.

Home is Newport News, Virginia, where his father is a plumber and contractor with his own business and his mother works in the mess at the naval base in Norfolk. He has two older sisters, one in the Coast Guard, the other in the Army. His father wants him to join the Navy, wanted him to go to the Naval Academy, or at least to do ROTC. He thinks he might quit school altogether and move to New York to audition. I want to dance, he says as he swivels back and forth in his chair, swinging closer to me each time until finally his thigh touches mine. I sit upright when he places his fingers on my knee and smiles. What about you, he asks. Your parents know, I say, the first thing I have said since ordering a glass of lemonade now drained on the counter before me. I play with my straw and stir my melting ice cubes until there is enough

...ter to drink. Again my mouth feels dry. Damien shakes his head. Does it matter, he says. I'm not there. Maybe I'll never go back. But you'll have to go back at some point. We all have to die at some point, he says. So what's your point? I'll deal with that when it's time. He squeezes my knee and points at the clock. The clock says I have less than ten minutes to get to practice. I search my pockets for the twenty-dollar bill my mother gave me for gas this morning. Don't worry, he says, I ate a salad before you came. But I owe you, I say. Next time, he says.

There is no one to tell how his eyes really are green and that Damien has incredibly smooth lips and killer dimples. There is no one to laugh with about his cookies and milk, to gush to about the fact that he is eighteen like I am eighteen only he seems much older. He has more facial hair which he keeps perfectly trimmed and he works two jobs at two different sports stores because no one is paying for his college but him. There is no one to talk to about waiting for his call because I've told him not to text me ever, and feeling my heart stop when my phone rings, and it's his voice, and again when an hour has passed and our words have filled our ears and still not enough has been said. There is no one to speak to about my headache and my stomachache when I leave my bedroom and encounter this beautiful prison that my parents have built, when I see pictures of me on the walls and side tables that bear no resemblance to the me they cannot see. Sometimes I stare at the family that owns me and I wish I were a different person, with white skin and the ability to tell my mother and my father, especially my father, to fuck off without consequence, and sometimes I stare at the white cards of Bible verses Reverend Olumide has gifted me and think that there is still a chance to change my ways. When we sit in his office, I talk to him about my future, about college and possible careers. I say nothing about the rest of my life so he thinks his pronouncements and prayers are working. I flex my abs while he speaks to force myself to breathe through the nausea and the pounding in my head. And when I leave I call Damien so that he can tell me it gets better.

Can I see you, I ask. I'm not invisible, he laughs. It's our joke now, just like the end of the bar is our spot now and that two hours between lunch and track is our time for cookies and milk and quick but soft brushes against each other's knees and bare arms. When I touch him he smiles. When he touches me I jump and look around to see if anyone has noticed. I am nervous, but after seeing him, I hit my speed workouts harder and Coach Erickson is pleased. After seeing him I don't think too much about Meredith or the fact that I've seen her talking to Rowan after class more, and the fact that he likes to say her name in the locker room and talk about her ass. Meredith has no ass and she knows it too. We used to laugh about that when we still laughed about things together. Now our eyes sometimes catch but it isn't laughter we see.

She was my best friend I tell Damien as he eats his chocolate chip cookie, but now we don't really speak. I don't speak to anyone from my high school. Fuck 'em, I was like buh bye, Damien says, the world is too big a place. Except that I'm still in high school, I say, and it sucks to be surrounded by people who live for their silly parties on Friday nights. You mean what you were doing when I met you, he says with that wicked smile, that all-knowing smile and wall of teeth primed perfectly to hold back secrets, to let them go if they should choose. I'm just playing, Damien says, you can relax. His hand rubs my back. You can relax, he says, and his palm touches my face. There are first times. Seriously, he says. I say, seriously man you're in college, you're free, you don't know what it's like being trapped anymore. I go to school and it's just me. I go home and it's just me. But you come here and it's also me, he says. His hands are on my hands, on my knees that I bounce nervously. I look at the clock. I have to go, I say and begin to gather the books and papers I bring to make myself think that people, if they are watching, see this for something other than what it is, but I'm a senior and this is spring—work has lost its meaning. Did I say something wrong, he asks. No it's just, I'm just frustrated, this feels so odd, there is never enough time. It's not ideal. Then let's make more time, he says, and he gets up when I get up. Most afternoons he simply waves goodbye. Today he walks me around the corner to the alley where I parked my car. It is empty except for an agitated cat that circles a Dumpster meowing. I like spending time with you so I spend the time there is to spend. I like the way you feel but I know it scares you to feel me—sometimes it scares me too, he says. He laughs but I don't. So I enjoy the little you let yourself be touched, there's nothing ideal so I see no reason to complain. I have one foot in the car and the other planted firmly on the ground. Damien folds his arms over the door between us. The small diamond studs in his ears catch the sunlight. You think too much, and it makes you feel alone, he says. We're different, I can't not think and I'm no-where near as strong as you, I say. I can't just tell my parents, my friends, everybody to go away. What's left for me? Damien says, the world. His face is insistent. You're stronger than you think, he says with eyes wide and full of light, his brow arched and his lips pressed together. These are the fragments of a face that got me an Uber home and they are everything. I want to touch him, to sneak my fingers toward his fingers, put my hands on his hands and let my skin rub his skin. I want to put my lips to his lips, but my only experience with that is Meredith and I am still scared by the idea of being completely connected to something so separate, so much a part of something that is completely me and also not me. A kiss is the ultimate uncanny, Ms. McConnell said in class after we read *The Passion*. Simple and pure, driven by lust, a sep-aration that knows no boundaries. You are not fully yourself and yet you are totally self-aware.

Damien moves towards me and all I can think is, I don't want this door to be here, but nothing is ever ideal. His lips brush my lips too quickly for me to feel shame, too fast to feel indecent, too fast. Then everything is slow and I feel him fully, and my body stiffens, my body melts, and I want to say stop, but those salty lips, but that searching tongue. The cat meows. I bring my hands to my lips to see if they are still mine. They tingle and buzz. Oh my God, I say, I have to go. Damien doesn't say a word.

Sin is a slippery slope, Reverend Olumide says to me when I see him next. My hand goes to my lips because I think he knows. He sits on his couch with his legs crossed and his arm stretched across the backrest while I perch on the edge of the facing armchair. Of course he doesn't know and yet, he is still a Man of God, they can sense these things. There is a rainbow-colored mix of peanut M&Ms in the bowl on the table between us. Reverend Olumide holds a few in his fist which he pops into his mouth at regular intervals. It's like these candies I just can't stop eating, he says, you put one in your mouth, then you want another, and another, and another. Before you know it you've eaten the whole bag, your teeth are rotting and about to fall out, your mouth smells like decay, he says. They are so good, but it's my choice to walk the path of righteousness, or to not and continue to shuffle along in the darkness. That's God's greatest gift.

This doesn't feel like a choice. It never did. But now I feel like things are completely beyond my control. His kiss—I crave it. I need it. I think about it. Now when we meet we kiss frequently. We make out. Sometimes I kiss with my eyes open just to make sure this is real. It is real, but always so short. He tastes of chocolate chips on some days, ginger tea on others. I want to ask him what I taste like but I'm embarrassed. I keep Tic Tacs in my pocket and Listerine strips in the glove box. Sometimes he is delicate with me, tentative like he wants to see if I really want it. It drives me crazy. My neck tingles and my chest burns. I press myself to him. I pull him towards me and we tumble down that slippery slope on the secluded benches in the darker corners of Meridian Hill Park while the Guatemalans and Salvadorians practice their patriotism on the dusty soccer field in front of us. Other days when he has come from or doesn't want to go to a shift at work, he is wild, sucking away everything I thought I knew about the way I'm supposed to be in this world. I feel like a star caught in the gravitational pull of a black hole, unraveling, spinning under the control of some unseen force, torn into streams of fire forever spiraling, never to be put together again.

But I still take the white index cards Reverend Olumide hands me, and I mumble good morning and good night to my parents. I pretend not to notice Meredith pretending not to notice me, though she forgets herself and smiles at me across the room when Ms. McConnell talks about Teju Cole and the African Imaginary. She knows I know she has kissed Rowan. I want to ask her how he tastes, but I won't speak to her until she speaks to me. I also have pride.

We can feel summer and graduation. Adam dares the teachers by purposefully not wearing a tie. Rowan copies Adam and soon all the seniors are an army of defiance. We watch the underclassmen scramble home weighted down by backpacks full of textbooks and novels as they moan about papers they have to write and exams that we don't have to take. We lounge by our cars and skip class to make runs to McDonald's or the gourmet pizza place across from it on Wisconsin that everybody knows but nobody remembers its name. There are girls' school versus boys' school water fights where the boys try to get the girls' T-shirts wet but the girls are smart and wear bikini tops beneath their school clothes. Sometimes I participate when Adam says, yo Harvard, you coming, but mostly I slip away to Sportzone in Georgetown so I can spend time with Damien on his break. He works endlessly now because he wants to spend the summer in Los Angeles at a dance studio, perfecting his hip-hop. He shows me video after video of their choreography on YouTube, sometimes he tries to get me to do it with him in the park. See over there, I can be me, he says. I smile but it makes me sad. I haven't found any safe spaces. Damien says, you're safe with me. Until I'm not. He raises an eyebrow. With you I mean, I add. I dream about an internship on the West Coast, but there is nothing for me to do. I am not the president's daughter. I've never met a movie star. I barely watch television. We could live together in an apartment in Venice Beach, Damien says while he strokes my hand as we sit in the park by the Potomac River at the sundial in front of the Swedish embassy. The sunlight plays on the ripples stirred by the soft and silent current. We can have an adopted cat named Gordon, he says. He kisses me. He has to move out of his dorm and into a friend's apartment before he goes to LA. He says I have strong arms that should come in handy. It's just by Meridian Hill Park, he says, I mean if you want to come. I want to and I have nothing to do until track practice, so I say yes.

His dorm room is a mess and it's cold. Half-constructed boxes litter the floor. Overstuffed suitcases and duffel bags burp clothes from between zippers that refuse to close. There are no white curtains or white sheets or white walls. Everything is cream-colored cinder block with half-fallen posters of famous dance icons next to rappers and singers. His sheets have come off the bed at the edges and his pillowcase needs washing. Home sweet home he says. He says, fuck this place. Then he kisses my cheek. Don't you have to pack, I say. He puts my finger to his lips then he licks it and I am all shivers and uncontrolled sensations. There are first times and there is his bed, uninviting but available. I am not ready for this, but no time is ideal. And yes his hot breath, and yes his lips, and yes something else, that thing that I have that he has that despite all the perfection makes this moment feel somehow very, very wrong. His hands are on my butt and he grinds against me and I feel him stiffen and shiver. The slope is very slippery, Reverend Olumide says. But so is the feel of his hard, bare stomach now that his shirt is off and my hands can feel how it feels to be a dancer. It feels so good. But in eternity, the choices we make echo, Reverend Olumide says and I see my father's face staring down at me from above, twisted with tears. If there is eternity, I will certainly have hell to pay unless this is just me, truly me, and no stack of Bible cards can change that. But his strong searching hands, sliding lower, uncoupling the things that hold me in, wrapping themselves around me. Stop, Damien, stop it. Stop what? Stop that. But this wave that passes through me. I am possessed. It is everything. Stop, stop, stop. This is all wrong, all so wrong. What's wrong, he asks through his wicked smile as his arm moves faster. I push him back. No. Then he is not smiling and I feel so very exposed. What's wrong, he says. I should go. Niru, I don't understand. I have to go, I say, I just have to go. My head and my heart, my weak legs and the parts of me between now feel so drastically out of place.

Outside the world is still normal. The cars still honk at each other and people still sweat while waiting for the bus. There are pigeons and sparrows cooing and singing and turning their incomprehensible mating dances. Niru, what the fuck, slow down and talk to me, Damien says. Gravel crunches beneath my sneakers as I walk through Meridian Hill Park to my car. Slow down, he says, I'm right here. I didn't mean to, I don't know. I stop beneath a tree. I can't Damien, I say, I'm freaking out. My arms quiver. My legs shake. I can't feel my face. Was that too much too fast, he asks. I thought you wanted me to, I thought that's why you came—why did you come?

The fountain is in full flair, sending water down the terraces to froth in the lily pad pond below. From this point we can see all the way to the White House and all the buildings between, locked in place, unmoved. I came because you have showed me something inside me that I can't control, because now the world before with its rules and requirements is not enough, I want to say, but I cannot speak.

The first boy I kissed was a sailor, Damien says. He was a white boy, skinny as hell, he was nineteen and I was sixteen. He had just joined the Navy, but he had a girlfriend back in Missouri that he said he loved. He said he needed her, but he wanted me. He talked about her all the time like she was some kind of medicine, but he used to call me at night when everybody was asleep and tell me to meet him in parking lots. The first time we fucked it was in a parking lot in his truck. He liked to play trap music and I let him fuck me like that because I thought that's how disgusting I was, that it should hurt, that I should be ashamed, cause I was his sickness and she was his medicine. He probably fucked her on a bed of flowers for all I know, who the fuck knows anything, but I do know I ain't nobody's sickness. I've done that. I have to go, I say, I have practice. Well go on and run then, go on and run, but me, I won't be nobody's sickness. I don't look at him as I walk down the steps to Florida Avenue, but I know he hasn't moved. I'm not doing anything wrong, Damien shouts at me, I'm not, so fuck you if you want to be this way. Just fuck you.

His words chase me up Sixteenth Street. I speed without care for the cameras or cops, weaving between the slow rollers and the trucks groaning out towards the Beltway. I stop at church and park the car against the curb, leaving the blinkers on. We used to race up these steps as kids. Back then they seemed so tall and so many like they really could lead to heaven. Now they lead to a locked door that refuses to budge. I push and I pull. I kick. I curse. I say a prayer but the doors don't move, even as I stare up at the sign that tells me ALL ARE WELCOME, and plead silently to God for help.

A police car pulls up behind my Volvo and an officer shouts from his open window, everything all right. I turn around but the glare from the sun prevents me from seeing any faces. Yes sir, I say, just dropping something off, but I can't get in. Well there's no standing here, you've got to move on, he says. I nod and walk down the steps.

My mother is home, seated at the kitchen table when I get back. She is surprised to see me and quickly shuts her laptop as if she is doing something wrong. I know what she searches for because it pops up in the browser on the desktop in her study, the only computer I'm allowed to use. How to talk to your gay son about sex is one. The others are about drug dosages, support bras and Spanx, everything no son wants to know anything about. But it's hard to keep secrets in this house. Shouldn't you be in school, she asks as she smooths her hair back and pushes her glasses up her nose. She is fifty but has only started to gray at her temples. The wisps of silver make her look magical, like she combs tinsel into her hair. Her teenage patients say it makes her look like a pop star. Track doesn't start until late and most of my periods today are free, I say. She pushes back her chair as she stands and says, well are you hungry? My mother is not a small woman. She is taller than most other women and the thin frame of her youth is thicker now, not Oprah but far from Iman who she holds as an ideal for the physical form of a woman her age. When she begins to mother, she grows smaller and less intimidating. How did I give birth to such giants, my mother says as she passes me. She touches my cheek and then stops. She asks, what's the problem? Nothing, I say. Okay, she says as she moves to the fridge, I can warm some spaghetti, you people always say you want to eat pasta before you run, isn't it? I stand at the kitchen counter watching her fuss at items in the fridge and talk to something wedged in the very back. I don't know who keeps putting this thing back here, she mutters, it must be your father. She turns around with hands full of cucumbers and lettuce. Can you make the salad, she says. Mommy, I'm not hungry, I say. She says, anyway if you don't eat now then we can eat it with dinner. Skin these. She hands me cucumbers. And wash these, she says launching a box of cherry tomatoes to the counter. I rummage around the drawer for a peeler. I can't find it so I grab a knife. You're going to hurt yourself with that, my mother says. Mommy I can use a knife. Just use the peeler, she says, it's in the drawer next to the measuring cups. I didn't see anything there, I say and start on the cucumbers cutting the tips so I can peel back the skin in thin strips. We have not worked together in the kitchen for a long time, ever since my father made it clear he didn't think boys should spend too much time learning how to bake. I feel her watching me, hovering, her eyes reaching like desperate hands to steady my motions and prevent an accidental slip of the blade's sharp edge.

Sometimes I wonder who my mother might be if she weren't married to my father. Everyone around him seems that much less free-spirited, that much less open to possibility, so much more controlled. At her office, she is loud and filled with infectious laughter. Here she is more quiet and deferential. I can cut a cucumber, I say more sharply than I intend. She winces and busies herself with searching for the vegetable peeler if only to make a point. Utensils clatter as she sifts through metal and silverware in the drawers. Your father is always moving things around here, she says over the clink and clatter. That's because you just throw things in drawers, I say. But I know where I put them until you all decide to mess everything up. I say, I cook almost never so it's not me.

All I wanted was an empty house and a moment of quiet to process everything Damien has said. I thought I would be able to sit quietly at the kitchen table or even on one of the metal chairs on the deck facing the trees separating our house from the neighbors'. Don't be rude, my mother says. I'm not being rude. And don't interrupt me, she says in her voice that stops even my father midsentence. She turns to face me with her arms crossed over her chest and her rear against the open drawer. The lights above shine on spoons, can openers and stainless-steel measuring cups that OJ and I bought her for her birthday some time ago when we still had to ask my parents for money to buy them birthday gifts. I groan softly against my clenched teeth but she hears me all the same. She says, enough, enough, just enough. It's too much already, I've never—thank God—had a problem with any of my children, but now all of a sudden it's like you are three different people and I don't ever know which one I'm going to get. It's exhausting, you hear me, you are exhausting me. Can we not just have some real, genuine peace in this house? Between you and your father everyone here is always walking around like someone has died or someone is about to die. Or people are shouting or sulking or whatever it is you men do. You see my hair. You people are making me old! For once can someone not fucking shout at me for something, I say, I can't wait until I'm out of this stupid fucking place and no one can yell at me.

My mother's mouth falls open and her eyes lock on to my face. She has heard me swear before, on the phone when joking with friends but never have I said any such thing to either of my parents. Never. I have always assumed that such an event would result in my being beaten within an inch of my unborn grandchild's life, but she just stands there like a malfunctioning robot. Is anyone keeping you here, she says finally. If you are unhappy, please go. Go and find the place where you feel happy. I'm sorry, I say, but it's too late. I've fucked up. The less I've said the better things have been, the less likely my father has seemed ready to pounce on me for the smallest mistake. If she tells him what has happened, this might be the end. I'm really sorry. My hands smell of cucumber as I wipe my nose. She tosses the vegetable peeler in her hand to the counter between us. Its protected blades glint in the sunlight streaming through the large bay windows. Do what you like, she says. Mommy, wait please, I say. Get out of here, I don't want to talk to you. Not like this, in my house, my mother says. Her voice is flat and hard, her eyes fixed directly to mine. You should go and find whatever it is you want to find. Me, sef, I'm tired, I'm going upstairs, she says. I listen to her reach the top stair, enter her bedroom, and shut the door. It's just me now.

9

For some of us this is the end of a season, the culmination of three months' worth of gut-busting hard work, Coach Erickson says. It's hard to hear him over cheering from the bleachers as the track teams from rival high schools arrive and parents transform into fans and fanatics. The sun bears down on us. We sweat but haven't even started our warm-up laps. For others, it's the end of the road, the last time you will ever run competitively. Whichever one it is doesn't matter. Today we're going to leave it all on the track—every last drop of sweat, every ounce of energy—we are going to leave it here and we are going to take that title, Coach Erickson says. We all cheer because this is what we are supposed to do, but I know that everyone is nervous. The relay teams have botched handoffs twice this season. One of our high jumpers sprained his ankle playing pickup soccer. He wears sunglasses and a baseball hat with his sweats, but he's a junior, so for him there's always next year. I want to see personal bests, Coach Erickson says.

And if you're not racing, you're warming up or cooling down, and if you're not doing either of those then you're cheering your heart out for this team. All right bring it in. Adam.

Our hands stretch toward the center of a circle where Adam starts to hop from left foot to right foot while bobbing his head. We're on a new level he shouts. We're on a new level we shout back. We're on a new level. We're on a new level, he calls and we respond with more and more energy until we are all bouncing and shouting and the sweat starts to drip down our faces. We break into hoots and hollers, streaming towards the sun-baked orange track for our two team warm-up laps. According to tradition, seniors link arms and lead these last laps at the championship meet. I join my classmates at the front. Adam says, we're almost there Harvard, and rubs my head. Let's do this.

As we pass the packed bleachers where fathers have taken off suit jackets and rolled up their sleeves and mothers fan themselves with their programs, I notice my parents standing together amidst a sea of white faces. My mother wears a pantsuit, which means she has come from the hospital and my father wears dictator aviators while he holds his gray suit jacket folded over his arm. They wave when they see me, but my arms are locked between my teammates. I can only nod and smile. If my mother hasn't said anything to my father by now, she probably never will, but she still hasn't said much to me this past week either.

When we finish stretching I take a moment to myself underneath the large maple trees on the far side of the track. It's almost over. All of these people who have dominated my life ever since I became self-aware will soon fade away and there will be new people and new structures. I haven't told Coach Erickson that I'm not going to run at Harvard. Not that I don't see the point, but I'm tired of running in circles while thinking that I'm making progress. And yet it is progress. I can see the seconds and milliseconds shed from my time. I cross the finish line before everyone else, accept their smiles and high fives and fist bumps and then line up to do it all again because that's what I'm supposed to do. I don't want that life. Damien said I don't have to have that life, but we haven't spoken since I left his apartment and I'm too afraid to call.

We're still friends right, Meredith says. She stands over me in her black warm-ups with purple and gold stripes at the sleeves. Her hair is pulled back into a ponytail. She has a cartilage piercing in her right ear. I think it's new. I thought you weren't talking to me anymore, I say. She wears racing flats instead of trainers and she keeps bouncing to stay loose. I wasn't but then Rowan asked me to prom. Oh, that's nice, I say. I told him I was going with you. Please save me from that hideous creature, please. She sits down next to me, slips her arm through my arm and rests her head on my shoulder. I mean you can't already have a date or something, she says. I tried to talk to you, I say without looking at her, I sent you notes, I bought you candy. It was good, she says and also you can't draw for shit. I wasn't drawing for shit, I was drawing for you. Very funny, she says, so we're cool? Totally cool. You'll go with me? I don't say anything. Meredith stands up and dusts her hands off. I'm going to Barnard, by the way, she says.

I look up. She smiles. Wait, seriously? Congrats! I start to get up but she waves me down. You can celebrate with me tonight—Riverrun. I nod yes. Every senior goes to Riverrun and has gone for as long as track has existed. It's how we know the season is over. It involves alcohol and the Potomac River, and only seniors are allowed. The school hates it, but what can they do besides issue warnings to kids they can't really punish. I'll see you there, Meredith says before she jogs off to join the girls stretching in a circle on the grass.

I would much rather see Damien than go to Riverrun. I pull my phone from my bag and punch in his number. It rings but he doesn't pick up. I hurl the phone against a tree trunk. It bounces off and lands at my feet undented, unscratched. I am losing my pride, I tell myself. Niru, get over here, Coach Erickson shouts at me from the infield. I change into my racing shoes.

The moment before the gun goes off is always the most silent. Your world is quiet, but it is not calm. The runners around you bounce and flex and relax, flex and relax. They slap their faces for motivation, they look to the sky and mumble prayers to God. The coaches shout instructions and the teammates cheer as do the fans in the stands, but you cannot hear because you are somewhere else, somewhere deep inside, preparing your body to deal with the coming pain, the breath sucked from you, your limbs on fire and the voices that won't let you stop. They say keep moving, it gets better, it will be better if you can only break through this pain. They say there's another life after this torture, a new level, just keep breathing. Then the gunshot and your body no longer belongs to you. Yes, you are there, you are present but you are no longer in control. Whatever happens from this point happens and all you can do, all you must do now is breathe, keep breathing, don't lose your nerve, don't choke, no matter how much it hurts, don't stop breathing otherwise it will all be over before it's time.

They cheer for me. I can't breathe. Harvard isn't going to know what hit them, I hear. I can't breathe. We are the champions, I hear, we are the champions, they sing around me. I can't breathe. Your personal best by a long shot. That's Coach Erickson's voice. That's my boy. It's my father. It's like I'm dying, trying to hold on. My body says oh no, and my knees buckle but so many arms are around me, they hold me up. The voices they say breathe, keep breathing. They bring me water, they bring me something sweet and then they lay me down in the soft grass where I feel the blades against my tingling skin.

The parents mill about the bleachers and track to congratulate and collect their various offspring when the meet is done. My father leans against the chain-link fence separating the bleachers from the track, his shades over his eyes, sleeves rolled up. He smiles at me, a full-on I see you smile that must have only ever occupied his face at the moment I was born. He waves at me as I sift through seniors and our supporters speaking words of humble thanks and goodbyes. My medals hang around my neck. Our team trophy has passed from hand to hand as we take pictures so that later, when we have children, we can prove that we were once active and fit. My father doesn't have these pictures, he has the war, but he smiles all the same. He says congratulations, and holds his hand out to shake mine. I accept and his rough palms grip my hands tightly. Your mother had to go back to work, he says. She's proud of you, we're proud of you, I'm proud of you. My stomach flutters. My parents do not say things like I'm proud of you or I love you often—my mother more than my father, which is still almost never. They show their love by paying our tuitions, OJ says, and by putting food on the table. They show they are proud by demanding even more than you think you can do. OJ is coming for my graduation—his girlfriend too. He says he is proud of me, but he doesn't know me. When we get to the car, my father hands me the key, still smiling. He says, you should drive.

My father doesn't joke with his car, this Range Rover, a gift to himself bought a year ago the week after the board elevated him from COO to CEO. It is metallic midnight blue with deep brown leather seats and a grille curved upwards into a smug luxury-car smile. OJ had managed to convince him to let him take the car on runs to the grocery store, but no farther. I have sat in the driver's seat and fiddled with the steering and controls when the car was in the driveway, but nothing more. You're sure, I say. You know I didn't learn to drive until I entered university, my father says. The license plate shines in the sunlight under a glimmering Range Rover logo. My father's car has no stickers or decals, unlike my mother's Mercedes with its Harvard sticker peeling from the bumper. I couldn't afford to, what money was there to buy a car, my father says as he rests his hand on the side panel, then removes it immediately. The car is hot. I didn't know this, but I now file it with the long list of things he lacked growing up that he has given to us that we should be grateful for, like private school, piano lessons and family vacations to Venice and Prague and Rio de Janeiro. OJ says our father lives somewhere between the self-satisfaction that his success has made us soft and disgust that we are unacquainted with the brutal intensity of a world that he has effectively tamed for us.

Ngwa, ngwa, let's move, my father says. But as soon as we sit down, there are questions. Did you check that you're in park? But Daddy, you parked the car, I assumed you wouldn't—Never assume. Emergency brake, he asks. I push the button and feel a satisfying click. Do you know what all these lights mean, he asks. My father takes his Montblanc pen from his pocket and reaches across the center console to point at the dashboard. Okay, tell me. Tell you what, I say, now regretting not riding back on the bus.

You need to know these things. You don't want to be one of those people who just drives, that's what women do. A man should know what he's getting into, you should know what you're getting into, my father says. He's the kind of person who reads manuals for everything. Order and instruction, rules for this, laws for that, how-to diagrams and flow charts to show a clear path towards a clear goal. Maybe you should just drive, I say. My father says nothing for a moment before he shakes his head like he's shaking away a fog. No? He says, let's get going. My phone buzzes in the center console between us. It's Damien. *Ngwanu*, my father says, you can't be looking at your phone and driving. I pick up the phone and quickly slip it between my thighs. Then I pull out of the lot.

I learned how to drive with my mother because my father couldn't sit still. From the first movement forward my father's involuntary motions started. He chewed his lips while curling and uncurling his fingers on the armrest as the car gradually picked up speed. He tapped his feet and craned his neck to search for traffic and threats that I couldn't see. Manage the car, manage the road, manage my father, it was altogether too much work. Things have not changed. My phone buzzes again and I look down. You have to watch the road, my father shouts. I can't, I say, I can't watch the road when I'm too busy watching you. Well don't watch me then, focus on where you're going. I can't not watch you. My phone buzzes again. Who is calling you like this, my father asks. Here, give it to me, he says. If you can't focus then give me your phone. He reaches for my legs. The car swerves as I push his hand away. He braces with one hand against the dash and the other wrapped tighter around his armrest. I slam the brakes. We screech to a stop and the cars behind us on the GW Parkway begin a symphony of angry horns. Someone passing in the next lane shouts, the fuck is your problem, through his closed window.

You've got to pull to the other side of the road, we can't stay here, my father says. He presses on the hazard lights. I think you should drive, I say. Don't be ridiculous, let's get moving, we're causing a scene. No, I think you should drive, I say, I can't drive with you in the car, it makes me too nervous. Well you'd better learn cause you can't drive without me in this car. Now let's move. I say, no, I'm not driving, you should drive, that's what you want. I wanted to do something nice for my son, he mutters, I can't believe this. Why are you so, so—fine, come down from there. I put the car in park and engage the emergency brake. When the doors open, the honking reaches its full intensity. The car horns harmonize and clash in an improvised, syncopated rhythm.

You guys okay, a youngish red-haired soccer mom asks as she rolls by in her red Chevy Tahoe. Her sunglasses sit on her forehead. She has crow's feet and freckles near her eyes. Just a little car trouble, think it will be okay, thanks for asking, my father says in his clipped tone reserved for white people.

I pick up my phone and step out of the Rover. A long line of cars stretches behind us down the GW Parkway. The Potomac River uncurls and expands even as it wraps around the city and the Cathedral glowers down on us. Somewhere in this mass of hatchbacks and SUVs some mom is worried about being late again to get to her kid's Little League game, and some dad is worried about being late again to pick up the kids for their weekend with him under these new and still-strange custody arrangements, some Salvadorian with no papers but lots of drywall in the bed of his pickup is worried because each minute in traffic is a minute more of possible exposure to law enforcement and who needs that. They are all now taking their anger out on me. My father brushes by me and sits down in the driver's seat. Then I hear the hood pop and he walks to the front of the car muttering, I can't believe this.

I put my hand to my forehead and whisper the same thing. I want to shout, THERE IS NOTHING WRONG WITH THE CAR and then add a YOU FUCKING IDIOT for good measure, but I stand silently between the car and the sloping grass-filled median holding my breath. Will you get in the car please, my father asks.

I walk around the back and smile at the older white man tapping his fingers against the steering wheel of a late-model Cadillac. I open the passenger door, but I don't get in. I shut the door and then close my eyes. A moment later I feel the hood slam shut. My father theatrically dusts his hands. The back of his shirt is soaked through with sweat. You all right over there sir, asks another driver, a young white guy with shaggy hair and sunglasses.

I think so, my father booms back and then dismisses the guy with a head nod and casual wave. Niru, will you get in the car please, he says as he climbs into the driver's seat. He doesn't look at me as he turns his attention to adjusting the rearview mirror. I clutch the door handle and bounce on my toes. My calves burn. Get in the car now, he shouts. I can feel his anger vibrate against the closed window. What's wrong with you? Our eyes lock through the glass. He checks the rearview mirror again. It will never stop, I say. Carpe diem, I say. My phone buzzes. Niru just get in, get in and let's talk about this. He reaches across the seats to try and push the door open from the inside, but I press my body forward against it. I listen to the hot metal of the engine click as the car idles. I smell the exhaust from cars creeping slowly by. Their horns have not stopped. Their horns will never stop. My phone buzzes. Then I turn and run through the cars to the shoulder lane. My legs are so tired. My chest burns, but I don't stop. Just keep breathing, I tell myself. It gets better. Niru, my father shouts, please come back, talk to me. But there is nothing left to say.

PART II

MEREDITH

1

The day I return, a homeless man comes up to me as I stand looking up at the gilded ceilings and shield-bearing Valkyries in the main hall of Union Station. He smells of urine and drink. His white beard has red streaks from malnutrition. You look lost, he says, are you lost? I tell him I'm fine and rummage through my backpack for the first note I can fish out from the miscellany I dumped inside before I left New York. It's a crumpled and worn five that I hold out at arm's length with my fingertips. He only has a few teeth that wiggle when he smiles. His eyes water. God bless you, you have a good heart, he says before he wanders away across the patterned floor towards another traveler.

Are you lost if you know where you are going—just not how to get there? There is still no Metrorail service to Georgetown and taking a bus, taxi or Uber during rush hour means conjuring a level of patience with this city that I have never possessed. I stand in place weighing options while the transit goddesses stare down their unwelcoming disapproval.

But it's early summer and the sun still shines in the evening so I decide to walk the three miles across town through a place I no longer consider home. The Capitol Building squats atop its hill and the Washington Monument remains singular and unmoved, enjoying its prominence only because of arcane regulations that have stunted the growth of surrounding buildings. I had a high school teacher who used to tell us that the game is rigged with winners and losers decided long before the players have any choices to make. Ms. McConnell lives in Los Angeles now and writes for television. I wonder if she's happier there or just less oppressed.

I have never really liked this city. It was forced on me against my will by ambitious parents in search of greater opportunities and better lives. That's why everyone comes here, to this seductive monument to self-advancement or at the very least, self-preservation. It's a city that doesn't take risks. Men wear boxy suit jackets over golf shirts tucked into khakis. Women wear sensible skirts, pantsuits and pumps. They all pull roller backpacks behind them because of subway ads enumerating the signs and evils of scoliosis as they walk to big-box buildings made of similarly colored sandstone. You can't get lost here because there's nothing to lose yourself in. These avenues, at least downtown, are not built for wanderers, and these monuments are constructed to inspire awe not contemplation. But things have changed if only to protect the desire to remain the same. The streets have more barricades because the streets have more impromptu protesters, a dismal lot with their posterboard signs and hoarse-voiced chants against the monster in power and his minions. There are more armored vehicles now and more police officers in tactical gear and body armor wielding large black guns. It's a brave new world wrapped around the old one to make it great again. I think about my boyfriend in New York and how he wraps his arms around me when I have my nightmares—they are less frequent now but no less intense—or in the mornings when we are both naked and vulnerable and that vulnerability arouses him. Sometimes it arouses me too, but sometimes it is easier not to resist. He wanted to come with me because he wants to know where I'm from. I'm here now with you, I told him, but he says with me it's a case of the more you see the less you know. He wants to meet my parents, to see the house I grew up in, to smell the bedsheets of my youth. He's a poet trapped in a banker's body. He reads T. S. Eliot on the subway and slips index cards with lines from *The Love Song of J. Alfred Prufrock* into my pockets before he goes to work. My parents are moving, I told him, there is only so much change they can handle.

They are not home when I arrive. Mom has left a short note on the front door written in barely legible cursive that she insists makes sense: Dad and I waited as long as we could but we had to go to a dinner. I made some boxes for you and put them in your bedroom. Leftover salmon in the fridge. Love Mom. She could text but she doesn't text when she wants to make a point.

Inside there are boxes everywhere, in the living room and dining room, all open, some empty, some half-full. I drop my backpack on a couch and weave my way through the chaos to the kitchen, where the counters are covered in dishware sets that I never knew we had. A broom and mop lean against the refrigerator door. I try to hold both of them in place as I pull it open, but they slip from my grasp and fall to the floor with a clatter. The fridge is empty except for a box which contains the salmon. There is also some milk and a Brita of water. This must be heaven for Mom—she hates to cook. I warm the brown paper box in the microwave, fill a blue tinted glass tumbler on the counter full of water and stand with my back against the fridge feeling it vibrate and hum while I pick at the salmon with my fingers. The flesh is tough and rubbery. It needs salt, but Mom has already packed the condiments.

Leaving must be difficult for them, for Mom especially. She is the one with extensive social ties, the friends she plays tennis with, the boards she sits on, the professional women's groups she has started and grown. I wonder if my absence has anything to do with their willingness to move. Whenever we talk Dad says, this house is too large for two people, and since you never come home, what's the point of keeping it. They will move to an apartment in Cambridge, Massachusetts, courtesy of Dad's new job—a professorship and head of institute. Mom says she has always wanted to live in a place overlooking the river, even if that river is frozen half the year. She wanted me to come back earlier. It takes longer than you think to pack up a life, she scolded on the phone. But that depends on how expansive the life. Ever since I left Washington, I have tried to contain my world in the smallest space possible. Don't keep anything that can't be packed into two suitcases. Don't attach yourself too strongly to people or places. My boyfriend says I have commitment issues. When we argue, I tell him attachment and commitment are two very different things. Dogs are attached, humans are committed, I say. He wants to get a dog, but I'm not ready for that. Maybe that will change after they move and I'm really homeless.

Mom has left packing tape on a stand outside my bedroom. There is also a box marked DONATE in the hallway. She has never been subtle in her suggestions. It's not how she was raised, she reminds us. Her family is large and argumentative. They show and tell. Sometimes it drives Dad crazy. Otherwise my room remains untouched, the same framed posters—because Mom would only tolerate them if they were framed—the same creaky black office chair and a white desk with red drawers. Dad and I painted it when he still had time and I still had patience. It's the kind of thing a person keeps if a person keeps things. Mom said, you'll regret it, when I told her she should sell it on Craigslist or eBay. Maybe we'll put it in storage, she said. My grandchildren will thank me. If you have them, I mumbled, which she chose to ignore. Mom has opened my closet and placed a wardrobe box in front of years of clothes hanging undisturbed. They smell vaguely of cedar. I have no need for more clothes in New York so I pull what's in front of me from the bar without ceremony and prepare for a cathartic dump into the DONATE box. Then I see it hidden in the back of the closet where it could almost remain unnoticed, a blue-and-white windbreaker jacket with a little bit of shimmer. My breath stops as my stomach clenches and I am reminded in full force why I don't come home. Niru wore that jacket on the last day I saw him, the last time he came over to my house.

2

I am eighteen and I sit on my front steps with my legs pressed together at the knees against the urge to use the bathroom. It's silly to wait for him out here, bouncing puppy-like with anticipation for someone I have not really spoken to over the last two months but the idea of waiting fascinates me—these moments stacked upon moments to be traded for an experience that may never live up to the anticipation. I should go inside and relieve myself, shower and wash away the dried sweat and grime from today's track meet, but I don't.

Niru appears suddenly at the intersection with its slowly moving traffic, walking with the slight limp of a man who has just run for his life. He wears his blue-and-white warm-ups and as he approaches, I run through all the possible ways to stage a greeting. We aren't who we used to be. I can't touch him the way I used to touch him. My hands can't linger on his back. My head can't rest on his shoulder. When he reaches me, he rasps a breathless hello. His face is still fresh but his movements are deliberate and old.

I slide sideways towards the bed of ivy with leaves that cradle last night's storm water and pat the warm bluestone beside me. I reach out, pull him down by his hands and throw my arm over his shoulder. This seems acceptable. He doesn't tense or withdraw. We sit quietly and watch the sunlight slide across the houses towards the Georgetown University clock tower. It catches on the silver and chrome handles of cars parked against the curb. After a long while Niru says, I want to disappear, I want to disappear completely, gone, nothing, no trace, forever. Stop, I say and place my free hand over his mouth. His lips are sticky but I don't pull back. They'll sweep the streets tomorrow, I say. I feel his shoulders relax and my fingers grow warm as he lets out a long breath. They'll sweep the streets and everybody will park on the opposite side, no questions asked. What does that have to do with anything, he says. Nothing, I say, except that it helped you forget—for a second. I can't help you disappear, I whisper into his ear, but I can help you forget. I say, I will help you, and press my lips to the short, prickly hairs of his recently shaved temple before I take his hand and lead him up the steps to my front door.

The house is empty so it's just us. My parents trust me enough to leave for a weekend in New York—work, Dad said. And opera, Mom said. The track team wanted me to host something, but I've never liked the idea of many other people in my space, on top of the things I know, touching them with their grubby fingers, leaving unfamiliar smudges and scents. Sometimes it is better to go to the world than to bring the world to you.

We order a pizza and lie across the couches in the upstairs den as we wait for it to arrive. I make frustrated attempts to turn the thick pages of a coffee table book about Greece with my toes while Niru stares at the ceiling and pops his lips. He says nothing as his fingertips hang just above the fraying border of a faded blue Persian rug. The curtains glow with the sun and the room smells of the flowering trees outside. Dad's roll-top desk refuses to close over unruly document stacks, magazines and business cards. It's the only corner of this house where I feel like I'm allowed to be myself, he says sometimes, but mostly he ignores it and this room is totally mine. Riverrun, I say. That will be fun. It's finally the end, finally. Niru isn't interested in that line of conversation though he seems not altogether unmoved by the suggestion. His head rolls towards me. He puckers his lips and blows a sarcastic kiss before he turns away. He mumbles, all of those people, the same old people, the same old shenanigans, the same old jokes. But for the last time, I say, then never again if you don't want. Or what do you want, I ask. Something different, he says, something more real, or maybe I just want to disappear. What gives, I say, rising to my feet too fast so the world swoons. I fall back to the couch overcome by a very real fatigue and dehydration from the meet. I search for my Nalgene bottle on the floor near my feet.

Niru's popping stops. He swings his feet around too quickly and unsettles Mom's carefully arranged coffee table books. He doesn't look at me. His eyes come to rest on the scaled replica of John Trumbull's *Declaration of Independence* that I hate, that Mom hates, that Dad considers part of his freedom corner. He is patriotic but not sentimental so Mom and I think the placement is ironic but it stays because Dad sometimes feels like a minority in his own home.

Niru grinds his teeth, places both hands on his knees and sits up perfectly straight and lets out a wordless scream. Tears drip slowly from his eyes. I move toward him, drop to my knees and plant myself in front of him. The full blast of his breath hits my face and he refuses to look at me even when I place my palms on his cheeks, and then over his mouth. You're scaring me, I say. Niru I'm here with you, I shout and I shout everything I have heard said by people to people with too much pain. It will be okay, you'll get through this, this too shall pass, the last phrase being something a mom likes to mutter. The neighbors, I plead. His eyes say, fuck your neighbors, but then they say something much more terrifying, they say nothing at all. Can you see me, you need to stop, Niru please stop, I say from between his knees, please stop, you have to stop. I dig my nails into his forearms and thump a knee against the rug. Help me, tell me what to do, tell me how to make it stop, I say. This could just be one of his practical jokes, like that time he pretended to seize in front of me and gargled Sprite to make his mouth foam. I dialed nine and then one with sweaty fingers while I rubbed his chest and said, stay with me, before his arm flailed in just the right motion to knock my phone from my hand, before he laughed loud enough to fill the kitchen. I poured ice water on him for revenge, but his startled yelp couldn't match my cold trembling fear that made it almost impossible to hit the right numbers to save his life.

The doorbell rings. I say, I think the pizza's here, are you going to be okay if I go down to get it? He replaces a lock of my hair that has slipped from my ponytail back behind my ear. I dash downstairs to the door and impatiently thrust a tip in the delivery man's hand. I snatch the box from him. It's okay Meredith, Niru says when I get back. Everything will be okay. I just need to be strong, you just need to be strong. We sit at the kitchen counter with the box of Papa John's before us. I am still dumbfounded by his performance upstairs. I ask, are you okay? But of course, he responds in a silly imitation of a French accent, *mais oui, certainement.*

I don't press but he can see that I'm unsettled. I want to hug him, to hold him, but I also want to slap him until he can see that, objectively, his life is almost perfect. The world loves him; it takes him seriously; Harvard takes him seriously. I drag a pizza slice from the box to a plate and hand it to him. I was just letting off some steam, he says, sometimes there's just too much pressure. Well you're acting really weird, I say. Dude you've got to relax, the school year is over. All we have to do is literally stay alive long enough to graduate and then we get to go to college where life will be totally different. It's not that far away. Not for you, he says, you never have any real pressure. Hey, I say, but I don't say any more than that. I have always felt like he dismisses my problems because in his mind white people don't have real problems, just issues. He picks a sausage from his pizza slice and places it on his tongue. The boy I was seeing doesn't want to see me anymore and I just ran away from home, he says. Wait what, I say, slow down, there's a boy, what boy? He wants to smile the bashful smile of a person who likes someone but his eyes are sad. You didn't tell me about a boy. You didn't speak to me for a long time, he says, things change, but it doesn't matter, I have nothing now. Aren't we being a little dramatic? I left my Dad on the GW Parkway, ran away from him, from all that, I can't take it anymore, it's crushing me, it's too confusing for me to live all these lives when I only want one. I don't know what to say so I ask him if he wants water. I want to see him. Who Damien? The guy? He nods. Tell him to come to Riverrun, I say, but Niru raises his eyebrow and I suddenly feel stupid. Join that fuckery? With Adam and your lover boy Rowan? No thank you. He's in college. Oooh, sophisticated, I say with much more bite than I think I mean because something pinches inside my heart. I say, I can't believe you have a boyfriend. He is quiet.

Niru wants to go to a club or bar on Fourteenth Street because it's close to where Damien lives. I can call him and maybe he'll come, he says. I want to tell him he's dreaming but I don't because he's hurting and I want to be a good friend. You have a fake ID, he says, and I have my brother's license. Which you've never used, I say. He gives me the side-eye. He says, just help me with this, with eyes full of please and thank you all mixed together. But what about Riverrun? We'll go after, he says, and I'll buy you a drink if you come with me, something better than the cheap beer they'll have by the river, he says. You'll have to buy me more than one.

Fourteenth Street is alive with bodies by the time we get there. The weather is nice so people linger on the streets. There are women in short sequined or pastel shorts and tight short skirts, revealing tops and made-up faces. There are surrounding men who all look the same, awkward with shirts tucked into jeans or khakis that fall over boxy black or brown shoes. Their pale skin turns orange in the streetlight. If this is real life, I want very little of it but Niru wants it all. He charges ahead towards the bouncers at the busiest place on the street where the chatter from multiple meaningless conversations competes with Top-40 pop that beats against the windows and spills into the street. My hand shakes when I produce a license that I got because everyone else was getting one. It says I'm from Maryland, that my name is Amy, and that I am twenty-three years old. I don't look like I'm twenty-three yet because I don't wear my clothes and makeup with the same confidence as the women around me. My jeans are the wrong choice in this heat and I am unsteady in my heels, but my tank top is loose and I like the latticed straps that show my back. Guys do too—I feel their fingertips in the space between my shoulder blades every time I wear it to a party. They touch me now when they say hello. They offer to buy me drinks.

At first I say no because Niru stands next to me and even if he has his own agenda, part of me feels like it wouldn't look right. He shouts in my ear that his calls to Damien won't go through and he holds his old Nokia phone in a tense hand with flexed muscles that stretch the arms of the too-small golf shirt I produced for him from my father's closet. The bouncer didn't pay attention to his warm-up pants and sneakers; the track coaches are stylish enough to know that functionality doesn't always trump form. You go and find reception, I tell him, I'm a big girl, I'll be fine. I should be fine because this will soon be my life in New York, clubs with men my age and much older all circulating in search of something that I supposedly have to give, that I'm still supposed to guard furiously, that I tried to give to the boy who has just left me at the bar alone so he can give it to someone else I have never seen. And I am here to help him. It hurts even if nature always wins in the end. It hurts because loving someone is very often against your will at first and there is no amount of will that can change the situation before me. I have tried.

But I can also forget. Yes, I will take your drink, I say to the man with an ambitious smile. He asks my name with his beer breath and beautiful face and his dark, frat boy hair. His hands touch the skin on my back and I look around the room for Niru. Yes, I will take your drink, because I am a senior—even if you can't tell—and it's a Friday and why not live a little in this strange space of irresponsibility before we become real humans. He says things about things that don't register. My friend is somewhere here, I say. He's coming back, I think, I say listening to myself struggle with simple words and phrases. But he keeps on talking and Niru hasn't come back yet and I can feel my heart. I am always someone's accessory, someone's afterthought, the supporting actress in another person's drama and that thought fills me with fire. My parents leave me alone for the weekends because they have each other. My friends want to use me for my house. Rowan wants me because he thinks I'm less noticeable and therefore easier to fuck on prom night. And this bro with his wavy hair and his pale outstretched hand and his fingers that creep up my back, he wants me and that scares me but I smile. It's so loud. Maybe we can talk somewhere more quiet, he says as he pulls closer and his hands move lower. I can feel the part of him that wants more of me than I'm prepared to offer, but I wobble as I try to step away because I don't often wear heels. There are other bodies in the flashing lights and loud noise that bump against mine and his, pressing us together. Then there is Niru's hand on my shoulder and his body behind mine and his tearful eyes and that phone which he holds, still quivering. The frat boy notes the separation with a frown. Niru says, he's not coming, we should go, like now. But I'm not ready to go, I say because now it feels good to know that I can make someone forget their manners.

Niru grabs my wrist. I try to wave his arm away because I'm tired and with alcohol I feel better standing in place. Backlit and surrounded by the pulse and chatter, he seems taller than his full six feet two. He holds me tightly. Can we go, he says with eyes that say please and thank you. I'm not going anywhere, I say. Dude, she said leave her alone, someone says. Come on let's go, remember Riverrun, he says to me softer now, in my ear, ignoring the bristling bro behind me. She said to leave her alone. Please don't touch me, Niru says to this boy whose name I can't remember, or maybe he never told me. Or what, the frat boy says, and I can't believe this is happening. Niru, you're hurting me. Meredith we need to go. There is a half-moon of bystanders around us now, waiting for something to happen so they can tell each other, re-member that time when—he was like six four—dude, he looked like he just got out of prison—total thug—complete felon—yeah. There are no bouncers but there should be bouncers for moments like this or maybe I should just go with him, with his hard eyes and now terrible face, his clenched fists and set jaw that the room treats with extreme wariness. I watch him play through events, the push and then punch that will surely follow, the scuffle and then the bouncers and police that will surely come. Am I worth it? To him, I'm not worth it, so he stands down and says, fine Meredith, have fun before he turns and walks away.

I should let him go and let this strange night be the end of a long and strange year that we will talk about when we are older at reunions when our lives are far enough apart that we can only share memories. But I can't. It would be easier if he hated me, because at least then he would have to acknowledge me, the way he acknowledges Rowan. He always seems indifferent to me. He is unaffected by my naked body, unmoved by my years of silent longing, so unconcerned with my well-being that he would leave me here with these wolf packs of young men. I try, but I can't let go of the fact that he left for Nigeria, and when he came back began to phase me out of his life. I pull away from the frat boy who clutches at me and asks if I'm okay. I start after my so-called friend, through doors on to a street filled with people and the smell of street food, pizza, alcohol, bodies. I see car lights, streetlamps and changing streetlights and it makes me dizzy. I hear too much happiness and laughter buzzing in the air around me and it makes me sick. Niru isn't far ahead now, just a few paces with his steps still smug even after that momentary humiliation. I feel so unsteady that I think I'll fall. I shout his name as he turns the corner into an alleyway and then I surge the way I do in a race or on runs when the competitive jerk in him picks up the pace and I don't want to feel inadequate. When I catch him midway down the alley, I push him from behind with a force that carries us forward to the ground. He is on his feet in an instant. I feel the full strength of his hold as he lifts me up and pushes me against a wall just beside a Dumpster. The smell makes me nauseous, but the pulse and throb of the music blasting from inside feels soothing. It's so loud I can't hear myself screaming but I know I'm screaming. I try to scratch at him. I try to slap him. I try to knee him in his groin, but he puts his full weight into holding me still. His body presses against mine as he mouths, calm down. Meredith, calm the fuck down. He bleeds from his face, from the pavement burn.

Then I hear it and he hears it—the heavy whomp of a siren. The light from a police car shines brightly against us and a metallic voice booms a tinny instruction. Step away from the woman and put your hands in the air. I can't see fully into the light but I know there are people there behind the open doors, crouching low for protection. Niru steps away from me with his hands held high. There is so much space between us now. My hands reach out across the space. Then he hears it and I can just hear it but the person behind the lights can't hear it because of the noise from the club and the noise from the street drowns out the Satie melody that says someone is calling you. He reaches reflexively, and they reach reflexively and he hears it as I hear it but he feels it and I don't.

He lies there in my father's shirt, limbs askew, sneakers still pristine white as his black blood pools in potholes and his hands slap against the ground.

You're safe, a voice tells me. He can't hurt you. Don't look, it's all over, it says. Shots fired, shots fired, requesting ambulance to alley between S and T Streets for suspect down. I feel cold. I become a series of shivers. Then I can't feel myself even as all the pizza and the beer, and whatever else frat boy decided we were drinking erupts from my mouth onto the pavement before me. I have no words now, only piercing sounds.

3

Mom is already awake when I come downstairs in my spandex shorts and sports bra. She stands in the center of the room surrounded by boxes, holding an old book in one hand and her glasses in the other. Oh hi, sweetie, she says when she looks up, Dad and I didn't want to wake you, you were just passed out on your covers. Her eyes drop to the silver bar in my belly button and her jaw tightens. I pierced it the summer before my senior year of high school and it has been a sore point ever since. Mom can't articulate why she doesn't like it and I can't say why her discomfort pleases me so much, but we have learned to live with each other. You're up early, I say. She spreads her arms wide to the room and says, so much to pack up, so little time. I thought that's what you pay movers for. They can't decide what you take with you, what you put in storage, and what you throw away, she says. She folds her hands over her stomach. Her ring catches the light while her glasses hang loose from her fingers. She has more splotches on her arms and more wrinkles now despite the creams and cleansers she uses. Everyone says I look exactly like her when she was my age, the same large eyes, the same dark hair, the same skinny, long-legged frame, but we can't be more dissimilar. We are an experiment in nature versus nurture. She is from Texas. I am not. She has five siblings. I do not. She paid her way through college and law school. I did not. She is methodical. I am not. We used to snap at each other without end, criticizing and reacting until Dad made jokes about being Switzerland. Now we agree that distance is better for some relationships. Mom says, you're sure it's not too cold outside, the mornings are still a little chilly. I'm going for a run. I know but—Mom I'll be fine. She opens her mouth and sighs. I can feel her eyes on me as I slip out of the front door and down the front steps.

The streets are empty and quiet this early in the morning and I can hear my own footsteps as they fall. I can never forget the imperfections in these brick sidewalks, where they rise and dip around tree roots, where loose segments can make you stumble and fall. Mom is right, the morning is cooler than I expected, but I am committed to the cold air sting that will soon turn to an unbearably soggy heat. Such is the way of a city built on a swamp. My boyfriend doesn't understand my obsession with running and I can't explain to him why I take a pair of running shoes with me wherever I go. He used to pout when I told him that I like to run alone. He said, you don't think I'm fast enough? No, I said, but we ran through Central Park together all the same and I purposely pushed the pace to prove my point. Abuse is what he has called it and it wouldn't be too strong a term, but I crave the feel of burning air struggling up my throat, the feel of my heaving chest. I pay special attention to each breath. He understands now and settles for kisses before I leave and when I return, but he always wants more. He says he will train for the New York City Marathon this year. He wants me to run with him.

In this section of the city, all the streets are corridors between pretty houses sloping towards the Potomac River. I peek into first-floor living rooms and kitchens and the lives just beginning at this time of day. That my parents are leaving, that they have sold their house, is all the more remarkable in a zip code where people cling to even the smallest property as their lifeline to relevance. It's a statement about how things have changed. This was once a city of possibility and hope. Now it's a society of fear no matter how colorful its row-house façades. I run to the sundial at the end of Thirtieth Street and watch the river churning this early morning. I love the Georgetown waterfront in the summer—especially the mornings when the only other people here are die-hard runners hell-bent on exercise before work. I follow the water's edge as the sun rises over Mount Saint Alban and flashes against the skyscrapers in Arlington on the Virginia bank. I run past the empty outdoor tables at the Sequoia and the Washington Harbor, thankful for the quiet and the cool breeze off the silver-blue water. Farther up, the river gurgles and makes petty rapids against slick rocks where small sticks struggle to keep above a white froth. There is already traffic on the Whitehurst Freeway heading from Maryland into downtown. It provides a steady background hum to which I time my breathing. I can feel the breeze against my stomach, and my thighs. My legs feel stiff and they tingle but I push forward towards the C&O Canal.

The first time we ran here Niru and I made plans to meet halfway between our two houses. It was a weekday in June the summer before senior year, long enough after the end of school that the novelty of boredom was wearing thin. That's like more than six miles for each of us, I said. You scared, slacker, he texted me. I hated his taunts. He said, you don't think you can make it, do you? Oh I can make it. Well prove it. I ran faster than I should have through the streets to the crushed-pebble path along the canal. At the ancient locks, water poured over carefully placed stones smoothed by centuries of flow. In the long stretches between, the water became stagnant and covered by a film of bright green algae. The sun that day was unrelenting. I wanted to stop but I pushed because Niru wouldn't stop halfway, and he wouldn't let it go if he overran me. He was the perfect partner during track season, always pushing the pace but making sure that his legs matched my legs stride for stride as he pulled me along by some invisible tether. I'd become a better runner because of our friendship, maybe even a better person. That was one of the things I'd written in the letter I'd planned to give him at graduation. But that never happened. As I ran farther into Maryland I picked up speed and brushed by other runners, people in pairs or with animals on leashes, all moving at a slower pace. I could feel my legs grow tired, but I kept pushing, my steps timed and rhythmic. I think up a song, Niru told me when I asked how he ran so steady, how he ignored the pain, and I play it on repeat in my head until I can't think of anything else. Then I don't feel and I'm free.

You tried, Niru said to me when I finally reached the halfway. He sat on a log by the path in the small shade of a scraggly tree. Here, drink up, he said and he gave me a bottle with water sloshing around a frozen ice core. You ran here with this, I said. Of course he did. Sometimes being friends with Niru was annoying. His deliberateness and conscientiousness stood in such stark contrast to my impulsivity that I had to remind myself that we were actually the same age. That's when I realized I'd left the house without my keys. Those who forget are often forgotten, Mom would say to me in the multiple text messages she used to send to make certain that one thing or another was completed at the house. I hated proving Mom right, but more often than not I proved Mom right. You can just come to mine, Niru said. He had never asked me to come home with him. My house was so much closer to school, and my parents were almost never around, so we had the run of the house most of the time. We sat at the kitchen table drinking juice and crashing through homework. Sometimes we watched YouTube clips on our phones—Niru liked Thug Life Animals—that was the only thing that could reliably get him to break focus. When my parents came home, they treated Niru with the politeness of functionaries used to meeting people they wouldn't remember but knew they would see again. He responded in kind with a timid formality, never speaking unless spoken to, and then mostly in Yessirs and Yesmaams before quickly slipping out the front door. I met his parents briefly after an orchestra concert where they sat in the front row with their eyes intensely focused on Niru and their arms folded tightly across their chests. His mother wore a loose blue Nigerian dress with elaborate gold embroidery along the cuffs and collar. His father wore a suit and tie. I didn't bother to search the audience for my own parents because I knew they wouldn't be there. After we finished, they congratulated us on playing as we stood together by the table of cookies, pastries and plastic cups of sparkling water, sparkling cider and juice. Niru's mother's eyes were half-closed behind her glasses. His father smiled at everyone but generally kept his conversations short. Your parents couldn't make it, Niru's mother asked when I followed them to their car after they offered to drop me at home. Will there be anyone at home with you, his father asked when we pulled up in front of my house. It was the only building without lights on. I could hear real concern in his voice. I liked him immediately despite Niru's tales of his strictness and intransigence. Your parents pay attention, I whispered to Niru. He shrugged.

We walked back to his place from the canal and I forgot my fatigue as soon as I saw the swimming pool in his backyard. I dashed to the wrought-iron fence, swung through the gate and catapulted myself towards the water. The cold made me gasp, but it felt good to have something wash away the film of sweat and salt from my skin. The chlorine stung my eyes and nose and my running shoes grew heavy with water. I kicked to the pool's edge and pulled myself up against the warm brick edging. Niru's bare feet hopped on the hot pavement before my eyes. You're crazy, he said. Then he jumped in.

We chased each other around in the pool despite our fatigue and dehydration. We splashed each other and took turns trying to see who could hold their breath for longer. We challenged each other to see who could lie for longer on the sun-heated bricks. I don't have sunscreen, I said to him. I don't need sunscreen, he said. We laughed and dripped from the patio to the basement bathrooms where Niru pulled large plush towels from the linen closet. We wrapped ourselves up to dry against the blasting cold from the central air. His house was immaculate with thick carpets on the stairs and brightly polished wood floors and wood cabinets in an expansive kitchen. Piles of mail stood in neat stacks on a low kitchen counter next to small picture frames of his family in various places around the world. He scurried about nervously, adjusting this and that to make sure everything was in its place, sweeping a plate of uneaten toast into the sink, replacing an orange that had rolled off a stacked fruit bowl. I lifted lids from the two pots still on the burner. One contained rice and the other a thick vegetable stew that smelled of fish. Niru pounced and covered the pots. Then he lifted the stew and carried it to the stainless-steel fridge. Yo, I'm hungry, I said. You wouldn't like that, Niru said, we can just order a pizza.

You have a very nice house, I said to his mother when she came home from work. The artwork is beautiful. I ran my fingers over the embroidered tablecloth on the kitchen table. This is very cool.

Niru's mother chuckled and smiled. I like her, where did you find this one, she said to Niru, who stood awkwardly by a small indoor tree fiddling with its leaves. On the path by the river, I said, we went for a run earlier. People's parents always liked me. I knew how to charm adults. Because I'm an only child, I told Niru, because I'm more sophisticated. I loved the political conversations that swirled around Mom and Dad's dinner parties. I would lodge myself at the top of the stairs when their friends stopped by and listen to them talk about their marriages and divorces and mortgages and second homes.

You must join us for dinner, Niru's mom said as she retrieved pots and pans from her cabinets and vegetables from the fridge. She wore shiny red flats with her long light blue skirt. She had a playful band of colored hearts on her right wrist. When Niru's father came home, we all sat at the kitchen table and ate large plates of jollof rice and plantain. I was hungry so I dished myself a second helping, careful not to spill anything from the platter onto the deep-purple tablecloth. His father was astonished. It's not too spicy, he asked. He removed his tie and rolled up his sleeves. His mustache held on to tiny drops of water from his glass. Niru shifted in his seat when his father asked me about my father and the president. He stroked his beard when I talked about the Oval Office and the White House grounds. Niru's mom offered me more water and asked if I wanted ice cream. I always wanted ice cream so we ate dessert while the sun unraveled above the shifting trees in the backyard, until Niru's father asked, do your parents know you are here? His shirttails had slipped out from his pants. I said, no. I don't have my phone, I said. Niru's father shot a glance across the kitchen. *Ngwanu*, give her a phone so she can call her parents, he half shouted. It's getting late, Niru can take you home. I didn't say anything, but I didn't want to leave.

How have I made it this far? When I stop, I feel the full force of my breathlessness. I know these streets but I am unsure of how I arrived here. Each house on this tree-lined cul-de-sac stands as an island in a sea of impossibly green impossibly level grass, except for one at the very end where yellow dandelions pop up in random spots and clusters. I place my hands on my knees as I search for breath. My legs vibrate and my joints throb from the run. I should turn around and go home, or find a shaded spot where I can sit and wait for an Uber, but my feet move me forward, slowly. There are water marks in concentric parabolas on the white paint underneath the gutters and the black paint on the shutters has faded and peeled. Blinds cover each window. From where I stand, I can see the front door is ajar. I freeze in place as a man emerges with his chin tucked to his chest. His unkempt hair is completely white and frizzes like a halo around his head. He walks a few hesitant steps to the Range Rover idling in the front drive, opens the door and steps a foot inside while holding himself steady on the frame. Suddenly he leaps out and dashes back to the house, then back to the car which he finally backs slowly down the drive. It abruptly stops and he dashes to the house again, fumbles at the lock, disappears inside and closes the door behind him, leaving the car running. It sounds like it needs servicing.

Six years have passed, but I can still feel the police car vibrate beneath me. I feel things more than I see or hear because I don't want to see and I don't want to hear over and over the pop, pop, pop, pop—yes four—his hands slapping the pavement, his horrible, rasping breath. I don't want to see that officer's shell-shocked but determined face. I feel so cold, then hot, and I feel someone's jacket on my shoulders and a wet towel wiping my mouth. I feel my fingers stick together with blood that is not my blood and stick to a phone that is not my phone even though I hold it like it's my life. I feel the voices as they try to comfort me. They ask me if I'm hurt. They say an ambulance is on the way. They ask for identification but my card says I am Amy from Maryland. They keep repeating Amy as if saying that name will make me feel less alone. But Niru is no longer with me and I am very alone. This world is flashing red light and blue light and menacing silhouettes. I want to scream as they take me away from him. Instead, I close my eyes.

Then I cannot open them fully because the light is too bright. It makes my head hurt especially where Niru slammed me against the brick wall. I see people as blurred shapes swimming around in a shower of fluorescent light. I focus on voices and touch, slowly parsing this blip from that bleep, curtains sliding on aluminum rods, and footsteps from nurses whose sneakers squeak differently from physicians' clopping shoes. I hear different flavors of Caribbean accent and think of my childhood nanny Ms. Simpson who always smelled of cinnamon and roses, who wiped my nose in a way that made me sneeze. I hear different flavors of African accents that Niru's friendship has made easier to discern. Where is he, where is he? I ask the various people who enter my pod. They respond with some version of the same platitudes—everything will be okay, you're safe here—before busying themselves with the cold compress against my forehead and the different machines and monitors around me. They say, get some rest but when I lie back I can't breathe. When I sit up, I can't think. My stomach fights against my lungs and my throat burns deep in my chest. There is a tube in my arm secured by white tape. My legs rest beneath a white hospital blanket. I have no shoes. If there were ever a time to cry, that time is now, but I can't figure out how.

Where is he?

I know one answer, that he is not behind the next curtain, a drunken shout away, and that means something very bad. It means I didn't get to say, don't close your eyes, please hold on, stay with me, as people who are close to people say in all the movies. It means I will never tell him how much I love him. I didn't know a person could bleed out so fast but I never knew how fast people bleed when shot. I remember an Iraq war veteran who spoke to us at a school assembly. It's not like the movies, she said. She wore a black, formfitting mini dress that revealed a titanium prosthetic attached to a muscular leg amputated just above her knee. I got hit in the back too, she said and turned around to reveal a mottled budge of scar tissue in the deep scoop of her backless dress. There is no describing that pain, she said, all you want is to close your eyes and have everything be over.

A nurse says, this has been ringing. Her name tag reads Moyo and she hums religious praise songs while she works, taking vitals, inserting lines. She holds up a clear plastic bag with a few accessories, my small black purse, my iPhone with a freshly splintered screen and Niru's black Nokia that sings Satie. I look at the screen. It says DADDY. I answer because the word makes me feel calm. Who is this? Meredith. Oh Meredith, hi, how are you, Niru's father says, trying to sound normal, but I can hear worry and rage inside his extreme calm. I want to speak but can't find words. My lips stay closed, sticky with my own dried saliva. Meredith, are you there, okay good, where is Niru, is he there with you? I struggle with the sound of his voice as I push my brain to do the work necessary to open my lips to give the right response, any response. Are you there, okay well if he's there with you, tell him that we really need to speak with him, his voice cracks and I can resist no longer. I clutch at my hair with a free hand forgetting the spot where my head hit the wall and wince. Nurse Moyo catches the phone as it slips from my hand, ever ready as if she's been through this moment a thousand times before. Sir, she says, your daughter is here in the GW emergency room, she's in good hands, and she will be fine. I can't say much more but it's better that you come. Her face crunches, your son, hmm, I'm not, I don't know, hello,

SPEAK NO EVIL

hello? She looks at the phone for a moment and places it on the bed next to my legs. She says, he'll be here soon, I'm sure. I hug my knees to my chest and struggle to catch my breath.

Then he is here, all of him so very present. He is not calm. He does not wear a suit. His navy-blue golf shirt has large pink wounds from an encounter with the wrong kind of laundry detergent and it is only half tucked into wrinkled khaki pants. They have already told him. I know because he can't breathe. He gasps for air as he stands supporting himself with one hand against the wall that flanks the bay where they placed me. I struggle to slide upwards against the angle of the bed and the pillow behind me. Niru's father fluctuates in size and is sometimes more an abstract shape than an actual thing and that is just fine. A clear view to his shattered face patched and held together by sheer force of will is too much in a situation that already surpasses superlatives.

What have I done, I think. I clench my teeth and bunch the sheets in my hands. Meredith, he manages to say before he slumps against the wall and crouches down to the floor. He starts to cry and pound the wall with his fist. I listen to him and try not to watch because it hurts to look at things for too long and because Niru would have found this show of weakness unbecoming.

What do you say to a grown man in tears? Dad cried when his candidate lost the election. That is understandable—all the tense hours, all the sleepless nights, the thought that such devotion nearly cost him his marriage. Mom held his hand and I hugged him around his waist while we sat with a would-be senator that I wouldn't have voted for even if I had been able to vote. It's okay, Dad, there's always next time, I said.

With death, there is no next time.

It's all my fault, I say softly. If Niru's father hears me, he gives no sign. His shoulders shake. He clutches the back of his neck. It's all my fault, I say unsure what to do next, this is all my fault.

When he finally turns to face me with red eyes and a shining face, he asks, do your parents know you are here? I shake my head no. Well I guess we'd better tell them, he says, but he doesn't move.

4

Sometimes I wonder if my parents like me. I know the laws of
nature and genetic self-perpetuation demand that they love
me, but it has never been clear that I am integral to their lives.
They've had each other since Mom literally ran into Dad on the
steps of the Harvard Law library however many years ago when
Dad was adding a JD to his PhD and Mom was starting her first
year of law school. Dad wants to be a Supreme Court Justice, that's
why they moved to D.C., so he could clerk and then work at the
Justice Department, and eventually the White House, getting
to know the people he needs to know to be the next big thing.
It's why Mom has always worked in corporate America, because
someone must pay the bills—and then some. I don't know that
he'll ever make the Court now, the politics have changed consid-
erably and he's not getting any younger, but also there's me and
my baggage. In his most frustrated moments my boyfriend says I
think of myself too much. I don't disagree. I tell him that's what

happens when you date a younger woman and he is quiet. He says he doesn't get me, that I'm a mystery. Because I don't completely get me, I say. This current me is a young wannabe photojournalist trying to start a career in a world inhospitable to photojournalists, the kind of woman who has made certain choices in support of my ambition without fully understanding the why behind my ambition, who is too proud to ask my parents for money, but not too proud to stay on their insurance or to cohabitate, temporarily, with a man ten years older because I contribute in my own way even if he pays the rent—and besides Dad is ten years older than Mom. I know Mom disapproves because she doesn't ask about my personal life. Everything about me now doesn't fit her image of the strong woman. She has never relied on anyone to support her existence.

My life was supposed to be very different. Niru and I were supposed to go to Harvard together. He was supposed to become a doctor, the cool kind—a trauma surgeon who saves lives in difficult places. I was supposed to become a lawyer, the cool kind like Amal Clooney, who prevents genocides while wearing Louboutins. We were supposed to live in an apartment in New York, then a row house in Dupont Circle, and settle in Foxhall or Kalorama with our beautiful biracial children, an older girl and younger boy. We would name them Nigerian names and use our one car to take them skiing in Vermont. But then I kissed him and that loosely woven fantasy unraveled. Most of life since has been a mystery to me.

Mom and Dad eat take-out salads in the kitchen. Dad stands at the island counter in dad jeans and a T-shirt while Mom sits on the floor, her back against the fridge, legs stretched out in front of her, balancing a plastic plate on her lap. The biodegradable take-out bowl and two tall plastic cups of lemonade with mint leaves bunched inside rest on the countertop. Mom pushes kale leaves around her plate and watches the brown tail of balsamic dressing slide around the blue plastic. She spears a cherry tomato on her fork and brings it to her lips. Can you believe we're leaving, Dad says to no one in particular, but he looks at me. We're really moving on. Eat something Meredith, Mom says from the floor. You've been here how many days and I don't think I've seen you put food in your mouth once, I mean you can get something else if you're not interested. I use two black plastic forks to dish kale and chicken onto my plate. Dad squints because he can't see faces if he's not wearing his glasses. This was such the perfect place, he says. I remember when we first saw it, your mom, Texan that she is, thought it was way too small. Would have been too if we'd had more kids, thank God we didn't, says Mom. I guess I'm all you ever needed, I say. All we could handle, Mom says. Mom, I say. She sets her plate down and groans as she pushes herself into a standing position. Sweetie, she says, I'm just joking, do you want some lemonade? Now that we don't live together, she's much more affectionate than she used to be. Sweetie is a new thing. She pushes Dad's lemonade and a red plastic cup across the counter toward me. I'm going to miss this kitchen, she says, so much life has happened in this kitchen. For a second I think she's going to cry, but she doesn't. We've really got to get packing, she says before she leaves the room.

The balsamic dressing stings my lips. I slice into the chicken and watch its flesh separate around the plastic knife, releasing warm oils and a sweet smell that should be enticing, but my stomach is tight.

Niru and I spent the morning after he came out to me in this kitchen. We wore winter coats and wrapped ourselves in blankets huddling together against the gas oven because the blizzard knocked out the power and this was the only way to get some heat. It felt like the beginning of the end and the zombies might throw themselves against the glass-paned kitchen door at any moment. I asked, does it feel real? He said, I feel numb, I feel scared. So many people are gay Niru, it's not that big a deal, I said. That's just a dumb thing to say, nobody is watching you Meredith, nobody. Everybody is watching me. Then he laughed. I had to laugh too even if I hated him a little bit. Laughing made us warmer.

Now that we're leaving D.C. you'll visit us more? Dad asks. He sighs as if there is more to say that he doesn't know how to say. You know we're still your parents, he says, some things just don't change. Then he turns and follows Mom.

But some things do change. Niru's father has changed and that is at least partly my fault. I have also changed. I'm older and more sensitive now. I know more of the world. Maybe that makes me a better person, or maybe I just know more.

The next day I run back to Niru's house. Perhaps it's foolishness that brings me back here to watch the sprinklers spray a fine mist on either side of the black asphalt drive. It's why the grass remains a lush green even if no one tends to it. Sunlight bounces off the wet patches and the years of car oil trapped inside shine in intermittent distorted rainbows. I move towards the grit-streaked white columns at the front entrance and the old-style black lantern hanging beneath. Cobwebs stream from its rusted chain-link fasteners and it has no bulbs inside. Niru said his father liked the design because it reminded him of the White House. Now the luster is gone.

There are three packages on the steps, alongside a stack of old newspapers melting into a pulpy mass from rain and age. The potted plants on either side of the door have died and there is a forgotten coffee mug beside them filled with water and dead potato bugs. This place looks abandoned but I know his father still lives here. When I woke up this morning, my course of action was abundantly clear, a small voice said, you must go to him, and then nothing else. I bundled up Niru's windbreaker and left the house before Mom and Dad woke up. Now I am here, my finger suspended above the yellowed doorbell button. Stay or leave? That is the question. I look back at my tracks across the wet grass. The sprinklers chirp and whir relentlessly.

Six years ago, I come to apologize because that is the only thing I know how to do. There are numerous cars on the street and crowding the drive as their passengers linger in the dimly lit windows alone and in pairs, heads bowed forward, movements slow.

I can do this, I tell myself as the sprinklers spit and the night fills with a chorus of cicadas and frogs. They have told me to stay home, stay quiet, stay out of sight, but this feels like the right thing to do, that something good will come from public supplication to the mourners inside. A slow sad song muffles through the front door, off-key and yet still harmonized. I am still for a moment as sadness washes over me, then I press the doorbell. The light inside the plastic goes dark, then the noise, ding but no dong. I feel for the written note in my pocket. I have practiced its words multiple times in the mirror. I wipe my forehead with the back of my hand. My sneakers are wet. I have crossed the Rubicon. OJ answers the door. I have never met him in person, but Niru's stories and his pictures make him intensely familiar. There is no mistaking them for anything but brothers. Their eyes, their nostrils, their jaws follow similar curves and they both favor the simple sharp definitions of low-cut and freshly edged hair. He wears a simple white T-shirt distinctly stained in the two spots where it has been used to wipe now red eyes. The space between his nose and upper lip glistens. His face is blank as he searches my face, and then he realizes who I am. He opens his mouth as if to speak and his lips move but no words come out. I step backwards immediately forgetting the steps behind me, and unsure of my footing, I tumble down onto the wet pavement. Junior, I hear Niru's father say, who is at the door, before his body appears in the doorway. What the fuck are you coming here for, OJ shouts at me. Junior, it's okay, it's okay, it's okay, his father says. I push myself up to my knees. I have skinned my palms and both of my wrists are sore from the unexpected impact. I massage my tailbone with a free hand. Rods of pain shoot down my spine and into my legs. Let go of me, OJ shouts as he pushes toward me. Let me go.

I watch the two men struggle with each other, dark shadows silhouetted by the light behind. Niru's father holds OJ in a bear hug and whispers something into his ear while he bucks. There is little besides interlocked fingers and soothing words that prevent OJ from moving towards me with his full force and I swallow the blood trickling inside my cheek with a sense of relief. Still part of me wants him to break free, to hit me.

OJ sounds like Niru when he cries, a word here, a gasp there between soft moaning. Bodies fill the space behind them, dark figures crowding the doorway, jostling each other as they reach forward with quivering arms to pull them inside. Niru's father shouts, Ify as he steps toward them with OJ slumped against him crying into his chest, holding his hand away from his body like he is afraid of what else it might do. It's okay, take him, take him, please, Niru's father says, pushing OJ towards the arms which quickly pull him in. Please everybody, let's go back inside, it's okay, let's just go back inside. Close the door please. His shirt is wet where OJ sobbed against him. He pulls me up. His hands are firm and his palms rough. This close, I can see he has new wrinkles in his face and brow. Why did you come here, he asks. I came to say I'm sorry, I say. You're sorry? Young lady, do you hear what they are saying about my son? You think your sorry will fix that? It wasn't like that, I say, he never would have done that. He didn't like girls like that. Let me tell them he wasn't like that. He doesn't say anything. The door opens and a young boy peeks his head out. Uncle Obi, he says. Go back inside Chidozie, Niru's father says waving him away with his hands. He presses his palms together, puts his fingertips to his lips, and steps back. Do your parents know you're here, he says after a long while. No? I'll call you a taxi, he says, you can wait out here.

Six years ago I didn't know what I was doing, why I showed up, or how I even got here. Now I can answer at least one of those questions. I wait and press the doorbell again. No response. I knock on the door and it swings back from the seal. An alarm chimes sharply, startling me, then the house falls silent. Hello, I shout inside, Mr. Ikemadu, hello. I should turn back. I should leave this place immediately but my feet sink into a soft entry rug as I step into what looks like the movie set of an abandoned home. My steps creak across the wood floors as I pass a sitting room and dining room where the little light streaming through the drawn curtains captures floating dust that settles atop a large wood dining table. In the kitchen, a lopsided stack of dirty plates near the sink is a breeding ground for a swarm of flies. Stagnant water rests in the basin, covered by an oily yellow film. The trash stinks from its bin beneath the sink. I try to breathe through my mouth, but the smell is overwhelming. It owns the room. The paint on the ceiling bubbles where a leak has gone unattended and there are folded yellowed newspapers scattered across all surfaces, the place where mail once stood in stacks, the kitchen table where I once ate with Niru's family. I bring my hand to my mouth. This is what I have done.

I stand at the sink and look out to a backyard of full, green trees. Then I plunge my hands into the dirty water to search for the drain. It feels good to soak my hands in the filth, to root around for submerged cutlery and finally scoop away the leavings that clog the sink. The drain greedily sucks down water, leaving a yellow film clinging to silverware and burnt-bottomed pots. I begin to wash the plates in hot water. When I am finished, I empty a spray can of air freshener, cough and continue spraying until the scent of decay cowers under a nostril-widening lemon zest. We cleaned up the same way just before he drove me home that summer night. He was as efficient as a busboy in a restaurant, wiping the table with a damp cloth as he removed the place mats, as he handed me plates and saucers to scrape into the bin before ruthlessly rinsing them with the spray nozzle dangling from the faucet. If school doesn't work out, you could always be a waiter, I smirked.

I should leave before someone comes but I keep going. I have no idea what I am doing or when Niru's father might return. I should really leave now, but I keep going. Niru never invited me upstairs and despite having crossed the threshold of breaking and entering, it still feels sacrilegious to set foot on the carpeted steps that lead up and away from the kitchen. I remove my shoes and place them neatly to one side. I climb the steps between framed faded pictures of people from another time, in another country. There is a large black-and-white photo of a man and woman who can only be Niru's grandparents. They look uncomfortable in their fine Sunday clothes. Niru should be at rest now, hopefully at peace—permanently—beside their bones.

The top floor is a madness of boxes and bags spilling from a hallway closet left half open to display a disorganized collection of bedsheets and towels. I hear the high whine and low voices of a television so I move in that direction. The master bedroom pulses as images from a cable news program flash across a flatscreen. The remote control sits on a nightstand near a cascade of crumpled tissues spilling onto half-finished plates of food on the floor near the bed. A framed picture of Niru as a toddler lies on the floor next to an empty prescription pill bottle. I have already crossed so many lines, but this violation feels absolute. In every faith, there is a part of the temple too sacred for all but the most faithful. I back out of the room and close the door.

I have never been to Niru's room but I have seen pictures on video chat, the trophies garnished with ribbons, a poster of Kendrick Lamar hung next to a bookshelf overfilled with science fiction novels and comics, a large goatskin drum tucked away in a corner next to his clarinet case. I stand at the threshold of his room and look at life suspended. I hesitate to move my feet from the white hallway carpet to the green carpet that covers the floor of his room. I can go no further. There is a line between decency and the real world. There was a line between me and him before I kissed him, before he pushed me against the wall, before the pop, pop, pop, pop.

But you did not pull the trigger, Dr. Blake says. Repeat after me, I did not pull the trigger. She says, Meredith, I need you here with me now. I did not pull the trigger, I say, if only because I like her buzzed white hair and large black glasses. She makes me feel safe even if Mom and Dad forced me to see her. And breathe in, one, two, three, four, five she says, and release, she says. It's driving me out of my mind, I tell her. All the time, everywhere he's there watching me, waiting for me when I go to the bathroom in the night, when I turn a corner, when I'm sitting in the living room, when I run and I stretch and he should be there in real life, I can feel him, I can feel his eyes on me, I can feel him angry. What does it feel like to be watched, Dr. Blake asks. Oh my God, what the fuck, I want to scream at this doctor and her unending questions, what do you mean what does it feel like? I'm scared, I say, I'm really really scared. You think he's coming for you? Well yes, I do, I'd come for me.

But I'm not a monster, the police officer on television says to the heavyset black woman with voluminous curls. In the days after the shooting, it's all television can talk about, all the Internet can tweet. Niru and I are the subject of online laments and cable insult wars. The officer's eyes are afraid and he shifts from side to side in his seat. I saw what I saw. I saw a man attacking a young woman and I took appropriate action. She says, actually, this is a boy we are talking about, a teenager, a Harvard-bound black boy. She says, witnesses saw her run after him, that he left the venue before her. He says, I saw a young woman being assaulted and I intervened to stop it using what the department has deemed appropriate force. And you feel no remorse? A child is dead! But I'm not a monster, I'm not a monster, I'm just a police officer and a former veteran trying to do my best to keep our streets safe. There is the police chief on television, her blond hair in a bun stretching her shiny forehead, flanked by the mayor and some other officials of clear importance but little significance together in a small conference room arrayed against the cameras, the microphones and the invisible public beyond. They brandish words like tolerance and calm as if they are truncheons. There is no joy in this for anyone, she says and the officials nod their somber nods of affirmation.

I am also not a monster. But he won't leave me alone, he's in my nightmares and in my daydreams. You need to let him go, Meredith, Dr. Blake says to me as I hide my face behind my hands and sink into the armchair in her office. He needs to let me go, I say back as I hold myself and rock against the air. He needs to leave me alone, I say when I can suddenly feel his presence. He comes to me in the shower in the rising steam when I am naked, between the white tiles and sliding glass. Kiss me I say, but he doesn't kiss me and the hot water at our feet turns to blood so I scream, get it off me get it off me, and my parents come running with the things you say to people when you want them to be okay.

The morning of graduation I cannot get out of bed. The school has told me not to come, has told all the students not to say anything to anyone about what has happened. No one has called me. They all think I'm toxic or damaged, or both. I cannot stop crying so Dad holds me while Mom stands in the doorway with her half-open mouth and palms against her chest. Dad rocks me and whispers to me. He sings a little song in my ear as he dries my naked body with a towel while Mom stands in the doorway. He carries me to my bed, rests my head on his knees and lets my tears and snot soak dark spots into his white trousers. He says I love you, while Mom stands in the doorway. She blames me, I tell Dr. Blake, for fucking it all up for them, from day one. She blames me.

Breathe Meredith, with me, two, three, four, five, Dr. Blake says. I tell her, sometimes I can still feel him touching me, I can still feel his breath on my face and his face against my face, sometimes I can feel hands and sometimes. . . . Sometimes? Meredith, Dr. Blake asks as she always asks when I stop speaking. Sometimes I wish . . . What do you wish, Meredith? Sometimes I think . . . What do you think, Meredith? I think this would be easier if . . . Dr. Blake nods knowingly. It would be easier if he had raped you, she says. I look up like a cat caught knocking something valuable from a table. It's perfectly normal to have these thoughts,

Dr. Blake says. But I should have said something, I say, I should say something . . . I guess . . . You guess, Meredith? I guess . . .

Sometimes it's easier to be the victim, this woman says so matter-of-fact with her skinny jeans and her white blouse, and Mom and Dad nod like they agree. She is a PR crisis specialist sent by Mom and Dad's law school friend. I don't like her. There will be no social media, she says. You will not post, you will not message, you will not log in to your accounts—Facebook, Twitter, Snapchat, Google Plus—then she smiles like her cheeks are connected to hooks set to a precisely calibrated timer. We will say nothing, if you feel like saying something, you will call me or you will text me. And Mom and Dad nod like they agree. Dad, Mom, I ask but they don't say anything. Right now at least fifty percent of America thinks you were assaulted. That's good, I mean important, we can exhale a little, their sympathies lie with you. From here, the best way forward is just not to say any-thing. And Mom and Dad don't say anything. I'm not the vic-tim, I shout, he is. Meredith, Mom says, this isn't so simple. No one will—It seems pretty simple to me—Meredith, this stuff is too complicated for most people to—What's so complicated about the fact that he didn't assault me. I pushed him—You want to try to explain that to all those angry people out there? You think they—Mom, I plead, the police shot him. He wasn't trying to rape me. Mom, I pushed him. It was just a fight. No-body here is saying he's a rapist, the woman cuts in, we're just not saying anything, we are trying to draw as little attention to you and your parents as possible, there is nothing wrong with saying nothing. But they shot him, I say. They shot him, yes, the woman says, let them deal with that. Mom massages her temples with her fingertips. I shouldn't have pushed him, I sniffle. Dad rubs my back.

A phone rings and I jump. It is my phone. My phone is ringing. My mother. Niru's dad could come home soon from wherever he has gone. I should leave.

5

Our house is empty now except for the air mattresses we sleep on and the miscellaneous items Mom has deemed too valuable to entrust even to bonded and insured movers. We stand in the kitchen with boxes of pizza and a bottle of wine. Mom and Dad flip a coin to see which one of them has to drive up. The other will fly to Boston to receive the truck. Mom loses. Dad says he has no problem driving, that Mom should take the flight to Boston and he will bring the car. No, I want to do it, Mom says. Their little protests are too cute and echo through rooms with bright lights that have nothing to illuminate. Meredith and I can take a little road trip. Right, sweetie? Her voice drifts from the kitchen through the house to find me. I don't respond because five hours in a car with Mom sounds like four hours too many. When we get to New York, she will want to see where I live. They don't know that I live with my boyfriend. They've known precious little about how I conduct myself since I left their house.

I won't live with him for much longer. I'm moving to Portland, Oregon, or Austin, Texas, or maybe even Mexico City—at least one of those places is the first stop. I just haven't told anyone yet, especially not Mom and Dad who think I will take the bus or train to visit them every so often. Their laughter echoes through the house as they continue to flip the coin. With nothing of substance to absorb it, it bounces through these hollow rooms from wall to wall around me. There is no place I can't hear it.

My skin prickles. I am overcome with hate. They are good people for sure and they have always been good to me, which makes my emotions all the more confusing. They would say that everything they do, they do for me. They have paid for my educational pedigree. They will leave me an inheritance. If I want doors to open, they can open them for me. If I want assignments, the emails will come—willingly—because my father and my mother know people and the people they know always help their own. My boyfriend doesn't understand my reluctance. You're throwing away practical gold, he says. Just take one meeting, he says, just ask your dad for one introduction, it won't kill you, that's how this is done. It won't kill me, but he will never know the true cost. Mom, Dad, I'm going for a walk, I shout into the house. If they hear me above their laughter they don't say a word.

The humid night is heavy with an almost thunderstorm that rumbles somewhere far away while streetlights shine upon the stillness. I walk towards the Rose Recreational Center and the baseball diamond at the end of O Street. In the daytime Little Leaguers chase balls and each other and in the early evenings packs of dogs chase balls and each other, but this late, it's just me. I round the bases before exiting on P Street where I stop, tempted by the playground's shivering swings, but I'm not a kid anymore even if some days I sit and wish I was a kid again.

Life provides a graceful arc for the fortunate, Ms. McConnell used to say to us in class when our discussions veered off the subject of literature and into the murky slush of real-world problems illuminated in the books we read. My life has certainly been fortunate—with the obvious exception—and even then, I'm still alive. Most of its early stages are documented in leather-bound photo albums now in boxes rumbling northwards for their ultimate destination beneath the glass surface of Mom and Dad's coffee table. Nobody looks at albums anymore. Now they are a novelty form of memory, a nod to the immutable past at a time when things are so awful that we seek solace in revisionist histories. I can't forget completely, no matter how hard I have tried. Sometimes it works for a while. Some days this city doesn't exist, Niru doesn't exist and I am just me, separate, functional, independent and free. I feel like it's a betrayal to want many more of such days and yet I want more.

Ahead of me, Dupont Circle is a pulsing beacon of streetlamps orbited by red car lights. Water flows across the lip of its gigantic limestone chalice fountain set in the middle of a large stone bowl. The after-work crowd sits at its edges talking personal lives and politics as they always have, and always will. The rest bow their heads towards smart-phones and tap furiously as they grumble and navigate towards the intersections and Metro entrances. It all seems so very normal, like nothing ever happened here and yet this place was center stage for one of the largest impromptu protests this city has ever seen—courtesy of me—only I wasn't there. I have seen the pictures though. Even years later it's difficult to look at images of teenagers carrying placards with slogans like WHITE LIES COST BLACK LIVES scrawled in Sharpie, or at pictures of the performance artists naked, with iron collars and thick chains running from neck to neck, knowing that you played a major, if not definitive, role in this half-remembered drama. Now people have other things to worry about, like health care and jobs. We have always had other things to worry about.

But, do you really want to live in a world so closed, Ms. Mc-Connell asked us in class when we read *Invisible Man* and nobody paid attention. I remember her red face as she held her place with the book closed around one finger. No seriously, you all want to sit here, laugh and not pay attention because you think none of this applies to you. Wake up, you live in America, she said. It's not the sixties anymore, Rowan said. Ms. McConnell stood in the middle of the room red-faced, holding her book with one hand and her mouth with the other, holding her breath to regain some composure. Then she walked out of the classroom and the door slammed behind her. I looked at Niru for a long time but he didn't return my gaze. I looked around the room at my classmates for some sign of fear or shame but they were all blanks. After a few moments, I walked across the room to the door, and looked out into an empty hallway awash in silence. The women's bathroom was just around the corner a few steps away, but I couldn't bring myself to leave the room. I turned around to the thirteen other faces that looked at me asking what now. I looked at Niru who was texting someone. Don't look at me, he mumbled, I'm invisible.

I keep walking. I haven't been this close to where it happened, since it happened, even if I have searched for that alleyway again and again on Google Maps and street-viewed my way past the furniture shops and luxury apartment ground-level windows plastered with signs advertising thousands of square feet of prime retail space. In the daylight images, the stretch looks empty, manufactured and bored. The brick joints of the modern apartment buildings are too perfect for the restaurant with old western lettering advertising its "family owned" presence to the block and the boutique stores sandwiched between larger new retail outlets feel staged. But now, in the evening, when there are so many people, Fourteenth Street is alive. The thunderstorms still threaten but the cool air feels nice so people linger on the streets and on the outdoor patios. There are women in short shorts and tight, short skirts, revealing tops and made-up faces. There are groups of men who all look the same, awkward with shirts tucked into jeans or khakis that fall over boxy black or brown shoes. Some wear Converses or loafers and boat shoes with no socks. There are more police cars now parked and patrolling, but there are more police cars everywhere now for law and order, for national security. I make it to the intersection of Swann Street before I start to feel light-headed. There is nothing to stop me from continuing a few steps away from Fourteenth Street to the alley entrance but what am I supposed to do there? I have no wreaths, no flowers, no candles to light in his memory. I can't even remember his face, his real face, not the yearbook snapshot they used on television and in newspapers, Niru perfectly posed, his body angled one way with a manufactured smile plastered on his face as he looks at the camera. No one remembers him now no matter how many bodies packed the street to call out against his unjust execution. His death stains have long been washed away. I stop where I stand. My feet refuse to carry me farther. I am so tired.

When I get home, I find Mom seated against the wall at the far end of the living room bouncing a tennis ball off the opposite wall. She looks up when I enter but doesn't stop. There's a half-full glass of wine on the floor beside her which glows deep red. Oh hi, Mom says and throws the ball against the wall. It bounces back toward her raised hand and she catches it perfectly. Long walk, was it good, she asks. I nod. She bounces the ball against the wall again. She says, you don't have to drive up with me tomorrow, but I thought that maybe we could talk. About? Nothing, just talk, I mean it's been so long.

But how?

The last time we talked in this house, it didn't go so well. I had just come back from a long late-night run. Mom opened the door, still in her work clothes so her silver bangles rattled against each other when she moved her arms. Where were you, she said as soon as I stepped inside. Dad leaned against the wall by the stairs, grinding his jaw. I just went for a run, I said and started towards the stairs. Meredith, help me understand, seriously, why would you, at this point in time, go out without saying anything to either of us? You couldn't leave a note, send a text? Would it have killed you? Do you know what's going on out there, what would happen if those people—Those people, I said, cutting Mom off and raising my voice. That's not what I mean, Mom said. That's not what she means, Dad repeated. Well, what do you mean? Meredith, please, just help us here, we don't know what we'd do if anything happened to you, Mom said. I'm pretty sure you'd be okay, I mumbled. Dad pushed off the wall and turned towards me. Mom braced herself against the threshold separating the living room from the entry, biting her bottom lip. You've put us all at risk, Mom said softly, do I need to spell out what happens if—You mean what happens to your social standing if the world finds out that he didn't actually assault me. Watch yourself with me Meredith, Mom said, nobody told you to sneak into a club and get drunk. But you weren't here to stop me, I said. My voice trembled. Mom quickly wiped her eyes. And now you're making it worse, you're making it so much worse. Meredith, we're trying to help you, but you need to let us help you. Let you help me, this is all your fucking fault. Our fault? Peter, I'm not doing this anymore. No, Meredith, you are completely out of line. I won't have this in my house. You never wanted it anyway, I shouted as I moved to the front door. Mom grabbed my arm and held me as I tried to push past. You're not going anywhere, she said, every time you leave this house you do something else stupid. Let go of me,

I said as I dug into Mom's hand with my nails. She grimaced. I shook her arm furiously and pulled until she let go. Dad stepped forward. Don't! touch me, I yelled as I backed towards the front door.

Niru's father stood just outside, his face rough, unshaved and covered with small bumps. His lips were chapped even with this humidity. He wore rumpled slacks and a wrinkled white shirt. His shoes were covered in dust. He looked like he was permanently holding his breath.

My father doesn't bend, Niru said one afternoon when our homework could wait and the warm weather made him affectionate. He's always saying, "Straighten your back, square your shoulders, don't slouch, don't slouch or you'll end up an old man who looks at everybody's feet." But here before me was his old man bent and unable to support a heavy head, his pain now fully revealed, blasted out from deep within, mined, cut and polished to perfection. Meredith, he finally said. My name spoken from his mouth vibrated through my body right to the center of my chest.

Excuse me please, Dad said, can we help you? As a matter of fact, Niru's father said staring at me, I think she can. Dad tried to pull me back away from the doorway. Come on Meredith, he said. I let him pull me, but I couldn't move. You need to say something, Niru's father said. He stepped forward. You need to leave, Dad said, as he squared up and tried to move around me to the front door but I wouldn't move. Tell them my son is not a rapist, my son wasn't trying to rape you, that's not my son, you need to make that clear. Isn't that why you came to my house? You went to his house, Meredith, Dad said. She came to my house, Niru's father shouted. Your son slammed my daughter up against a wall—in an alley—Mom said from behind me. We need you to leave please, Dad said. And go where, Niru's father said. Where can I go? Do you know what people say to me, how they look at me? I am not the father of a rapist, my son is not a rapist. This is a difficult situation for everybody, Dad said. For everybody, Niru's father shouted, his accent sharpening his words. They echoed down the block. For everybody? Are you mad, sir? Are you mad? Is that not your child standing in front of you—alive? And you want to say for everybody? I'm going to call the police, Mom said. Please, go ahead, call them, let them come. If they kill me too, it will even solve all my problems. You people are something else entirely, you send your daughter to my house to what, to provoke me? Is that what you want, to provoke me so that you can call police and have them kill me too? His whole body shook as he struggled to contain his anger. His fists dropped to his side. All you people do, wherever you are in this world, is just bring death and destruction, you bring nothing good, nothing good but I came here because I know your daughter is not a bad person. You people have taken him and I can't do anything about that, but just give me something. Tell them what happened, he said to me, tell them who my son really is. Mr. Ikemadu, I said. It took a moment for me to recognize my own voice.

I wanted to say, your son liked to run his hands along rough stone surfaces and then feel the soft fuzz of frayed skin on his fingertips, your son reeked of Old Spice after track practice because he was too afraid of his own desire to shower before heading home, your son liked to put Nerds in his Coke and hated ketchup squeezed directly onto his French fries, your son admired you greatly and thought that the measure of a man was success and community standing, your son hated you because your love appeared conditional, your son wanted to punish you for your ignorance, your son was the most important person in my life and like you, I didn't know it until I knew. But I didn't say that.

I said, then we should tell them everything.

His father just stood there, blinking slowly.

Meredith, don't say anything, Mom said, just come back inside. Dad yanked me back with real force. I stumbled against him and his head hit the door frame. He groaned as he shut the door. I felt Dad's arms around me, squeezing me like he was afraid that I too could just vanish. Mom remained with one hand against the threshold and the other over her mouth, shaking her head. I can't breathe, I said to Dad. I felt nauseous. I can't breathe, I said, I can't breathe.

The ball hits the wall again. Lizzy, for God's sake, cut it out, Dad shouts from upstairs. We both find this extremely funny but we laugh quietly. I slide down to the floor against the opposite wall and Mom doesn't say anything. Normally she's anal about her walls, cringing when hands touch them, immediately rubbing out smudge marks and stains. Instead she rolls the ball across the floor to me. Maybe there doesn't have to be a reason, Mom says. Maybe not, I say and send the ball back to her. She pushes it back to me and I breathe in as it approaches. Do you want to move to Cambridge, I ask. It doesn't really matter anymore, she says. I really just want your dad to be happy, this will make him happy, I hope. What about you though? I'll be fine, she says, the firm has an office in Boston, so it's perfect. I thought you hated Boston? I do. Then how is it perfect? I don't know sweetie, but it will be fine. How do you know? These things always work out. Sometimes they don't, I say. Mom stares at me without blinking, then she shimmies herself up the wall, crosses the room and places her palm on my head. Her palms are as rough as they've always been but they smell of lavender dish soap. She says, tomorrow? I bounce the ball against the wall. Yeah, I say. Then I say, Mom, and she stops at the doorway to the sitting room, I have a boyfriend. That's nice, she says. She half turns back toward me and stares down at my face for as long as our eyes can hold each other's gaze. Good night sweetie, she finally says.

The air mattress is uncomfortable. Any movement causes squeaks or groans which echo in my empty bedroom so I'm forced to lie extremely still and listen to myself breathe. I stare up at the glow in the dark stars that sweep across my ceiling. They are faint now, almost nonexistent hints of fluorescence scattered across the darkness. Niru and I placed them up there together standing on stepladders arguing and laughing the whole time about the positions of celestial bodies. He wanted to use the Internet to map the desired constellations. I kept interrupting his placements with random planets and the odd rocketship. It was one of those things that seemed like a good idea at the time but in reality, made no sense. Mom was furious when she saw the stars. They were bright enough to make it harder to sleep, but she wouldn't let me paint over them.

I sit up and the air mattress squeaks. The streetlamps shine an orange light across the room that makes me restless and uncomfortable, but there are no blinds to pull. My backpack sits in the corner by the door. Niru's windbreaker sits on top of it. It didn't seem right to leave it in the house, on the steps, on his bed, especially not after I had washed the plates. I want to banish the ghosts, not resurrect them. I pull on my running shoes and shorts, grab his windbreaker and slip down the stairs and out the front door. Outside I slip my arms into the sleeves and let the fabric envelop me. The streets are empty except for the occasional car. I walk down the steps and when I reach the sidewalk, I run.

The ambulances at the George Washington Hospital rest quietly in their Emergency Room berths, siren lights dull and unimpressive beneath a blazing tribute to Ronald Reagan. Farther down, the Lincoln Memorial glows at the end of Twenty-Third Street, where the occasional white headlights and red taillights coming off the Memorial Bridge trace an arc around its base. We called it Riverrun because at midnight on the last day of track season right after the championships the seniors were supposed to meet at the track and run together through Rock Creek Park to the steps behind the Lincoln Memorial. The brave were supposed to jump into the water with their full tracksuits, shoes on to protect against broken bottles and rusty old shopping carts. Everyone would drink and sit on the steps until the sunrise talking shit about the future, maybe making out and drinking more. Niru and I argued about whether we would actually enter the water. There's all sorts of bacteria, there's broken glass and rusted metal, he said. I said, you only live once. That's some white people shit, he said.

I am out of breath by the time I reach the steps. The Potomac River is still and untroubled as it holds a vibrating reflection of the Memorial Bridge on its shimmering surface. There are small leaves and sticks idling on the water. I unzip Niru's windbreaker and peel the fabric away from my skin. Then I bundle it into a ball and fling it as far out over the water as I can. The jacket catches air, unfurls and flutters down with open arms onto the water's surface. It spins around next to the bank but refuses to float away. I stare down at it from the marble ridge. I sit and dangle my feet above the water before I reach forward and fish it out. I lie back, touch my head to the grass behind me and exhale. Arlington Cemetery rises up the hill across the river to where Robert E. Lee's mansion looks down upon the city. It looms above us in splendor surrounded by all the dead we cherish. I breathe slowly into the night air and watch as bright lights from the bridges and monuments wrestle silently on the river's surface.

I walk silently with the wet bundle beneath my arm. I have squeezed it dry, but it trickles river water down my side and my leg. I stop periodically to scratch my quads and calves. I am tired and the progress is slow, but I continue forward because there is only so much time.

Washington, D.C. is a different place late at night. This city sleeps. Its abandoned streets are silent as a world that is no more, where everything is an artifact. The houses cast shadows over the streets, the trees cast shadows over the houses, and the monuments cast shadows over it all to ensure that everything remains in its correct place. I'm happy my parents are leaving. Perhaps somewhere else I can help them build better memories.

The sky above has ripped open by the time I reach Niru's house and the colors spill across the clouds. His father's Range Rover sits in front and there are lights in the upstairs windows. The automatic sprinklers spray a fine mist on either side of the paved black asphalt as the cicadas chirp and morning birds sing. I cross the lawn without hesitation. He has removed the packages and the newspapers from the front entrance. I drape the damp jacket over my forearm and press the bell. There is a brief moment where I want to fold the windbreaker, place it on the floor between my feet and run away, but I don't. We have all been running for too long. I stand fast and listen for some sign that someone moves around within the house's darkness. Nothing. I turn around. Mom wants to hit the road by nine, once rush hour has ended. It's a long walk back and my legs are tired. Then the door behind me opens and I spin around to face Niru's father with his unkempt hair, wrinkled gray slacks and wrinkled blue dress shirt rolled up at the sleeves. He smells sweet like whiskey and sour like he hasn't bathed. He sways a little as he squints through the half-light at my face. I want to say good morning, but my tongue refuses to move and my mouth is dry. I want to say I'm sorry.

Instead, I stretch my arm forward so Niru's windbreaker hangs from my fingertips. He looks at me and then at the jacket. For a moment, he is completely confused. He says, you've been here before, haven't you? He takes the jacket from me and holds it up. He says, we've been here before, haven't we? He stares at me for a long while and says nothing. Then he says, well, go on now, speak.

Acknowledgments

Booksmay have single authors, but they are rarely ever sole endeavors. *Speak No Evil* is no exception. From conceptualization to cover, there are so many people who have enabled, encouraged, and influenced this story directly and through their friendship and support. While I can't name everyone who helped me move this project forward and I'm bound to unintentionally omit some names, I would like to thank the following people without whom this book is not possible.

TEAM *SPEAK NO EVIL* (OFFICIAL)

Jennifer—you are the world's most amazing editor. For your tolerance of tabletops full of index cards instead of pages of text, your willingness to endure long conversations over my patchy Skype or FaceTime connections from God knows where (yes Zanzibar), your quick responses to innumerable emails, your insistence that big books aren't always about page counts, and because you wisely wouldn't let me use "tho" in the preceding pages. I'm so very grateful. You also were not joking when you said four drafts. Now I know.

Jeff—your quiet persistence made this happen. We've now been working together for over a decade (see I'm old now) and with each year I grow to appreciate your calm, quiet insistence that finishing only comes with focus. For this and for taking a chance on representing a shy twenty-one-year-old so many years ago, thank you.

Tracy and Mark—there's a pond between us, but I'm no less grateful to you both, and Tim because you set it all in motion.

TEAM *SPEAK NO EVIL* (UNOFFICIAL)

Emma—you're far away but never truly far. If not for your timely intervention as I sat head in hands at a desk in Italy, I never would have had the courage to cut to the core of this story. Without your insistence that there was a good book hidden somewhere in the jumble of pages you read, I'd still be writing a novel about only God knows what. We both know I owe you so much.

Ian—WLA. These words—real words—are always real because of you. You know exactly what I mean so I won't say more.

Larissa—how amazing can a person be! There are people who read and there are people who READ with care, kindness, and page-numbered, extracted quotes contentiousness—literally. You and Philip (who first published my short story from which this novel takes its name) have been role models in writing and life since before I knew you. Now, it's the greatest gift to call you friends. Also that wood-smoked salmon.

Mary—you've spent the better part of eight years listening to me talk about this book in some shape or form, listening to me cry about it, whine, try to quit writing, not quit, and then try to quit again. Through it all you've been unfailingly optimistic and when necessary more invested in my writing than I could find the energy to be. I don't know where you get the patience to deal with me, but you've done far more than help with a couple essays in Butler Library demands.

Meredith—I will forever treasure our walk through Brooklyn Bridge Park when we sat on the steps and I read you the first bits of this book and you told me, keep going. Through our multiple musings in your studio I've learned so much about what it means to own my particular creativity from watching you work—and that has been key for making this book.

Ragz— *Du så denne historien. Du levde disse tegnene med meg og levde mine drømmer og mareritt om denne boken med meg til drømmene ble en realitet og marerittene falt bort. Du bøyer deg. Jeg skriver. Begge for livet. Siv—visdomsordene dine har hatt en dyp innvirkning på min sjel. Til dere begge har jeg verden på grunn av deg og deg. Jeg elsker deg.*

Steph—from tentative words before creative writing work-shops in college to lengthy catch-ups on the phone, I cherish our conversations about life, literature, and love. Your eyes on this manuscript, the hours we spent on the phone slogging through my characters' and my own motivations, the calming confidence of your voice, all while you were working on your own writing and a baby—my words are inadequate.

Zahra—you literally (he he he . . . I know not funny . . . but so so funny) listened to me read whole drafts of this book out loud and we are still friends. I don't think you can comprehend what that means to me. You've been an unequivocal force for good in my life and my work and I value your honesty like nothing else.

FRIENDS OF THE CAUSE

Elliot—we may be older, but your insistence in our days of youth that I should trust and do what feels right still means everything. Onyi—what would I be without eighteen years of our walking and talking through matters of the heart? Kayode—I have embarked on no missions without your strategic counsel and this is no exception. Thenji—you always listen when it matters, and you have always helped me find the truth. Robin—because you've said repeatedly the world wouldn't end yet and it hasn't. Robin—because your calm and caring have kept me alive since 2007 and because you introduced me to kale. Nell—there can never be enough molten chocolate cake outings with you. Megan—we will always have Bellagio. Dan—we will always have 478 CPW. Eileen—we will always have gummy bears on Bushwick rooftops. Purvi—because diamonds are forever. Amelia—because you can see a world I can't see and because you are bold in ways that make me more bold. Steve—because we know the world we want to live in, and we're going to make it happen. Annie—some of the best things come out of Park City and editing on the floor of your parents' house was perfect. Safiya—because you stay waking me up. Anjali—because our commitment to utter foolishness is the seed of true greatness. Ore—because you keep your promises even if I can't. Nayeema—

because we only just met and yet your words and encouragement were so crucial in that last mile. Sarah—because there will be more joint creativity to come for sure, thank you for your assurance. Charlotte—*parce que peut-etre que tu lirais ce roman*. Nedra—because Brooklyn neighbors can be soulmates. Ruthie—because the quest for creativity and cash-producing assets gets real. Julie—because ten years later we're still doing it in Africa, America, wherever, and you will always be a guiding light. Ines—because three words: Italian, hot, sauce, and because you are uncompromisingly direct. Dwayne—(my two-years-removed twin brother from another mother) because you know our city and for your eyes on a crucial chapter (and for your Facebook feed). RL—because you don't know it, but you made me feel differently and that changed this book for the better. Lauren—because your words, "it's not how pretty you look while you're doing it, it's whether you cross the finish line" have kept me in this race. Olivia—because you are so earnest. Adama—because, we can have that gin and tonic now, but really only one. Tamara—because you have helped me believe. And Sierra—because the struggle continues. To all of you and those not named, thank you most for listening.

Ventures Africa family—thank you. Building on Bond—(Esther and Len) I know . . . I know . . . the same damn thing every single day. But that charred kale salad tho. (See how I did that, Jennifer). Yaddo—you are probably the scariest place to write a book, but it worked out and the black guy (that's me) lived. Rockefeller Foundation Bellagio Center—you are the most beautiful place to write a book. Take me back. Radcliffe '12, stay representing.

MY FAMILY

Daddy and Mommy—I just want you to be proud of me. You've been so supportive and so encouraging every step of the way. I feel so lucky to have such wonderful, loving, caring, and invested parents. Your example is what I strive for, and I promise I will keep striving.

Onyi, Okechukwu, Uchechi—the world's greatest siblings. I have this picture of all of us from 1996 sitting on my desk that makes me so happy every time I feel down. I also just want you to be proud of me. More than that, I want you to know that I'm so so proud of all of you. Each one of you is an example of strength and creativity for me in a different way and each one of you makes me laugh with real joy in a different way. Andrew and Chioma—I love how y'all read my work faster than your other halves. For my purposes, they chose wisely. But really, you're two of a kind and I can't imagine life without you. Adaora, Emeka, Kelechi—I hope that by the time you are old enough to read this book, the world is a truly different place. Uncle Chi-Chi and Auntie Uju—we may not always agree but your wisdom is so important to me.

Beckett—Meow meow. Meow meow meow. Meeeeeeeeeeow.

IWEALA OUT

P.S. If at this point you're still reading, and you recognized the song references in the text, and you can figure out how to reach me, and you're not related to me—I don't know . . . I'll bake you cookies or something.

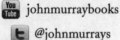
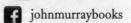